RAINFISH

Andrew Paterson is a medical doctor.
He grew up in a small town in Far North
Queensland, like the one where *Rainfish*
is set. He lives with his family in Cairns.

RAINFISH
ANDREW PATERSON

TEXT PUBLISHING MELBOURNE AUSTRALIA

textpublishing.com.au

The Text Publishing Company
Swann House, 22 William Street, Melbourne Victoria 3000, Australia

Published by The Text Publishing Company, 2021

Book design by Imogen Stubbs
Cover illustration by Cathrin Peterslund
Typeset in Stempel Garamond by J&M Typesetting

Printed and bound in Australia by Griffin Press, part of Ovato, an accredited ISO/NZS 14001:2004 Environmental Management System printer.

ISBN: 9781922330963 (paperback)
ISBN: 9781922459152 (ebook)

A catalogue record for this book is available from the National Library of Australia.

To Dad

1

THE WORST THING I EVER DID

MUM WAS AT work, Connor was in his room and I was dropping rocks down the storm drain at the end of our street. They ticked and tocked off the concrete sides on their way down. Sometimes you could hear water at the bottom, but not that day.

I pretended a baby had crawled in there.

Help, somebody help us, screamed the baby's imaginary mother, but everyone just stood around doing nothing.

Let's make room, ay? I said as I jumped down from my imaginary fire engine, then called, *Hang in there, brave little fella.* I jammed my arm down the drain as far as I could. *Reach out, mate, just a bit further.* My whole shoulder and my head were wedged in there. *Got ya. All right, mate, I'm gunna pull you up now.*

Hold on tight.

My head was stuck. I couldn't even turn it, and when I tried to move my shoulder it felt like it was dislocating. I pulled harder: lots of pain but no movement. The cool dark air caressed my face. I tried a not-too-loud *help*, and heard it echo down the depths of the drain. The actual fire brigade might have to rescue me. The whole street would be standing around laughing at my bum sticking up in the air. It'd be on the news: '*Local idiot gets head stuck in drain.*' I pulled back again; my head felt like it was swelling, getting stucker and stucker. Then suddenly I was out. My shoulder and chin were scratched but I was free, and that felt great. I realised there was nothing to stop me doing whatever I wanted or going wherever I wanted.

I knocked on Oliver West's door to see if he wanted to go for an adventure before I remembered he was visiting his cousins in Ingham for the whole holidays.

I started following the gutter looking for money—a kid I knew once found five dollars in a gutter—but I didn't even find five cents. No surprise: the people on my street weren't the clumsy-with-money type. I turned left and left again and then I was on the street behind ours.

It was so hot and sweaty no one else was outside; the

houses and the blue sky were my personal kingdom. I could have walked right through town and out onto the highway with the cars zipping through the cane fields on their way to Cairns or maybe Sydney. I started singing—and not just to myself either, out loud: *Thri-llerrr, thri-ller ni-ght*—but I stopped when I saw a boy coming along the gutter on the other side of the road.

His face glinted. He was wearing glasses. It had to be Connor's friend Damon: no other local kid wore glasses. (Connor wore them but only when he was reading.) Apart from the glasses, his walk gave him away. He walked like a gunfighter, arms hardly swinging, palms turned in towards where his holsters would be. Like he'd practised it in front of a mirror. I felt the urge to turn and run, but in the end I just stood and waited.

Soon there was only the road between us.

He said, 'What was your name again?'

I'd always thought kids with glasses were wimps, but he wasn't like that. He had freckles, big caramel blotches all over his face right up to his lips, and a cool Transformers digital watch like the ones they sold for $30 at Mellick's.

'Aaron,' I said. 'What was yours?'

'Damon. What's Connor up to?'

Connor was my big brother. 'Reading a stupid book, probably,' I said.

Damon took a cricket ball from his shorts pocket, tossed it up high and caught it. 'This town's so boring I'm gunna kill something.' Damon was new to Fingleton.

'Yeah,' I agreed, trying to imagine what a big place like Townsville, which is where he came from, was like. Probably had skyscrapers. Traffic lights. McDonalds.

'*Astonishing* how boring,' added Damon, repocketing the ball. 'May as well go to your place and see what Connor's doing.'

'Or we could go and catch guppies in the swamp behind your place,' I said hurriedly. 'There were some fantails there yesterday.' Fantails are those big guppies with rainbow-coloured tails.

He squinted at me. And then, to my surprise, said, 'Come on then, let's go.'

We were walking side by side like mates. I tried to copy his walk; from a distance we might have even looked like brothers.

Connor had told me I should stay away from Damon because he had done 'illegal things'.

I said, 'What's the worst thing you ever did?'

'I can't even tell you,' said Damon. 'You wouldn't

sleep for a month if I told you.'

The stones along the side of the road spiked our feet. In Fingleton kids wore shorts and T-shirts and no shoes—shoes were for stuck-up kids. I watched the houses we passed, hoping someone I knew would see us, but no one did.

Damon said, 'One time I had a fight and I put the other kid in hospital for a month, and that's not even the worst thing I did.'

'Wow,' I said, trying to think what I could tell him if he asked me what the worst thing *I'd* ever done was, but he didn't ask.

The way to the swamp was through the vacant lot next to Damon's house, which the council only remembered to mow every few months; in between times the grass grew high and people dumped tyres and empty paint tins there, and once an old fridge.

We picked our way through the grass. There was no fence to mark where the swamp began, just a line where the council stopped mowing, where the knee-high guinea grass changed to shoulder-high guinea grass.

'Definitely croc country,' said Damon. 'Hey look, see how the grass is all bent? A croc's been through here. Uh-oh, it's a bloody *huge* one.'

He was watching me while he was saying this, but

I suspected the stories about crocodiles in the swamp were made up to keep kids out, and so I just shrugged and said, 'Is that right?' And, gritting my teeth, I led the way along the thin track, brushing the grass away as I went.

We came to a dirt bank two metres high, which we slid down into a small clearing. It was surrounded by tall grass on one side and on the other by the reeds that grew along the creek. A concrete drainpipe, half a metre wide, protruded from the bank.

'Not a bad spot, ay?' I said.

The clearing had a private, secret feel about it, though from where I was I could still see Damon's backyard fence. I'd often thought of building a cubby house there and had even drawn a plan once: five storeys with a fireman's pole to slide down. Damon was looking back towards his house.

'Let's see if there's any guppies,' I said.

The creek was a tea-coloured, oil-slicked, luke-warm, mostly ankle-deep trickle. Through the reeds I could see some guppies tickling the surface with their tiny mouths.

'There's some huge ones,' I said excitedly.

Armed with an ice-cream container I'd left there the day before I eased into the water and immediately sank shin deep into the muddy bottom. When a guppy came near enough I sprang, landing with a splat.

'Watch it,' said Damon, wiping his glasses.

'Sorry,' I said as I scrambled out.

We peered into the container, now full of pee-yellow water. There was a fantail and a baby and an almost-transparent prawn.

'You can keep them if you want,' I said. 'I'll let you. You can put 'em in a fish tank.'

'Nah.'

'Or just a big bowl or something.'

Damon stretched his arms. 'I'm goin' into town. You can come, or you can stay here.'

'What about the guppies?' I said, but he just walked off. 'Wait, I'm coming.' I poured my catch back into the creek.

'You got smokes at your place?' Damon asked.

I'd washed the mud off my legs, and was walking soggily beside him. 'I don't think so.'

We did, but I'd never smoked. I'd never even been to town without an adult.

'I'd kill for a smoke,' said Damon. 'Let's see if we can find one in the gutter. Or I'll have to bum one off someone.'

We were on Shoe Street, which was like the other

streets in our suburb, with lots of houses that were basically wooden boxes on stilts, with front stairs and back stairs and sometimes a spare room under them like our place had.

Shoe Street was a main road for local kids but I avoided hanging around there for three reasons. Coldy's place was the first reason. Coldy was in my class. His mum and dad worked on fishing boats and spent months at sea. Sometimes they took Coldy along. Getting rocked by ocean waves all day while eating nothing but baked beans and getting home-schooled by his less-than-Einstein parents had curdled Coldy's brain. He was always eating people's glue sticks, stuff like that, to get attention. For some reason he'd bar-nacled himself to me—maybe because I lived so close and had been over to his house. If he saw me in the playground or on the street he'd follow me, be right at my elbow, watching me with his fish eyes.

Their ute wasn't in their driveway, which probably meant they were fishing, which meant I was in the clear.

The second reason, hidden behind a neatly clipped hedge, was the only one-storey house on the street. A witch who cursed people to death and disappeared neighbourhood dogs lived there. She could change the colour of her house whenever she wanted. People called it the Magic Red House, and it was bad luck to even look at it, but there it was, white, and looking as innocent as a house could. I'd seen the witch hobbling stiff-kneed in her front garden, and I'd once smelled a meaty, tomatoey smell there: dog stew according to Coldy.

The third and most important reason to avoid Shoe Street was Stevie Harmison. Stevie had blond hair and the kind of turned-up nose that made girls pass little notes to him in class. He was famous for having jumped off the Henry River rail bridge which was so high it would've made a Hollywood stuntman think twice. Stevie was a bully. Once he'd chased me up a tree with a cricket bat and hadn't let me down for half an hour—all because I'd said *you* when he'd asked me what I was looking at. He was in grade ten, a year above Connor who was in grade nine, but for some reason he never picked on Connor.

'The houses here suck,' said Damon. 'Our house in Townsville's got three storeys. Everyone on our street's a millionaire except us. The richest person in this whole town wouldn't be able to buy a house there. *Everyone's* got a pool. Proper in-ground ones, not plastic ones. My ten-speed and all our cool stuff's still there.'

Looking round I saw with Damon's eyes the broken toys bleaching in the front yards and the fallen-down letterboxes. He stopped in front of the Harmisons', the envy of the street with its tinted windows and wall cladding white as a new Porsche, but he only seemed to notice the pile of junk under the house, which included a broken ping-pong table (I could picture Stevie kicking its legs in after losing a game) and a life-sized cardboard cut-out of a girl in a bikini from a beer promotion. Damon shook his head and walked faster, like he couldn't bear to be around such crap houses.

On the whole of Shoe Street we found only two cigarette butts and they were thoroughly smoked.

'I bet you're wondering how come we live in such a dump now,' Damon said.

His house *was* a dump—worse than our place, even.

'It's 'cause my dad and my gran had a fight and she kicked us out. But they're gunna make up soon and then I won't have to stay *here* anymore.'

We crossed the road and cut across the oval that St Rita's Primary School shared with St Rita's High School. The oval had a concrete cricket pitch at its centre and in one corner a cricket net under a giant fig tree. Living so close to school was good because I could wake up at eight forty-five and be at school by nine—earlier if I didn't have a shower.

'I bet you got in lots of trouble in Townsville,' I said.

Damon had picked a grass stem and was sucking it like it was a cigarette. 'When I got caught. I was in a gang called the Evil Deads and I was the leader. I made a rule that to get in you had to have a fight with someone and you had to win. We used to do night raids: that's when you go out in the middle of the night when everyone's asleep and smash windows and steal stuff, do break-ins, stuff like that. At school we used to go behind the toilets and have fights and smoke all the time. I bet you never smoked.'

'I want to.'

'Well, you will today.'

We passed the high school, crossed School Street and were at my old school—I'd just finished grade seven—three concrete double-storey blocks together in a C shape all painted cream, the inner bit of the C being the courtyard. It was eerily quiet, but the stale-lunchbox smell was the same as always.

'I bet you know everyone in this school,' said Damon, squinting like it was too small to even see. 'That must be weird.'

'It's sort of boring. Are you good at schoolwork?'

'Yep. Especially maths and physics. You probably don't even know what physics is. They teach it in grade twelve. It's about electricity and space and stuff. When I was in grade eight, me and another kid at my school used to finish our maths early so they taught it to us so we wouldn't get bored. Which one's your old classroom?'

It was on the top floor of the middle block. We climbed the stairs and looked through the glass louvre windows at the plastic desks and chairs facing the blackboard, the statue of Jesus on the cross, and our paintings, which were still Blu-tacked to the back wall. I thought better of pointing mine out: a flame-mouthed dragon I'd been *so* proud of. It was attacking a stick-men's castle while the stick men ran about saying, '*Aaargh*'.

Damon crouched down and began pulling at one of the glass louvres.

'What are you doing?'

'Seeing if any are open.'

'Why?'

There was a loud grating sound. Anyone within a hundred metres would have heard it.

'That's loud,' I said, but he kept doing it.

Breaking and entering is what the police would

call it, which was a step up from my previous worst thing I'd ever done—killing our classroom goldfish by pouring chocolate milk into the tank. I wasn't ready to jump straight to criminal offences. I had to do something.

'There's someone coming!' I hissed.

He stopped, and we both listened, but there was no noise. He looked up at me, eyebrows raised.

'Probably a security guard,' I said. I was lying: I hadn't heard anything. 'They patrol here on holidays,' I continued. Another lie. I was pretty sure they never patrolled.

'So where is he, then?' said Damon. He slid the louvre out of its holder and leant it against the wall.

'You can fit through there, right? You're smaller than me.'

'Nah, I don't think so,' I said, though I knew I could. 'Unfortunately.'

People went to prison for breaking and entering. Maybe they'd let me off with parole because it was my first offence. Stop being pathetic, Aaron, I told myself. You made the security guard up. We're not going to get caught.

It was at that precise moment that I heard the loudest noise I'd ever heard in my entire life.

2

TREASURE

SMAAASSSHHHH!

Instantaneously we both sprinted down the stairs and out into the playground and threw ourselves behind a bush.

'Whoops,' said Damon once he'd got enough breath. 'I accidently kicked the louvre over.' He started to laugh. 'You should've seen your face.'

I was puffing too hard to say anything.

'Bet you never ran so quick before, ay? You pushed me out of the way.'

I shrugged. His eyes narrowed. 'If you want to hang out with me, you can't be a chicken.'

'I'm not a chicken.'

He nodded like he was saying, *sure you're not*.

We took the hedged lane that led between the

school and the church, which was a copy of some old church in Europe. Its doors were open so we stuck our heads in. Blue and red light filtered through the stained-glass windows, and clear light from the small windows around the dome high above the altar, but it was mostly dark because of the shadows from all the pillars. We could hear the faint sound of town traffic.

Damon stepped inside. 'Hello,' he called, and *hello* echoed to the top of the dome, circled and then echoed right back at us as loud as when he first said it.

'*Ssshhh*, Damon,' I shushed. 'You're not supposed…'

We sat on a pew. There were candles in the candle stand and flowers in vases beside the altar, which was like a dolls' palace made of marble.

'You see that bowl thing?' I whispered. 'That's holy water. You dip your finger in there and put it on your forehead.'

'And if you're a devil worshipper it burns you, right?' Damon said.

'Yep,' I replied. 'Or if you're possessed.'

'How come you know all this?'

'Our class does religion every Thursday.'

'Do you believe it?' he asked.

'Mum says church is a man-made institution. But some old people believe it.'

'What's through there?' Damon pointed to a door behind the altar.

'That's where the priest comes in.'

'I'm havin' a look,' he said. And with that he got up and walked down the centre aisle, then he turned and said, 'Coming?' as loud as day.

I scampered to join him. 'You have to whisper. Someone'll hear us.'

'No one's here. It's the holidays. Who goes to church on a holiday?'

The door was small and wooden with flaking paint. Damon turned the handle a few times but it didn't open.

'Must be locked,' I said, trying to sound dis-appointed.

'I think it's just stuck,' said Damon, and he rammed his shoulder into the door.

Whack!

It was so loud, I thought there's no way he'll do that again.

He did it again. *Whack!*

And the door sprang open in a cloud of rust.

'Huh. Maybe it was locked,' said Damon. He stepped inside, and reluctantly I followed.

Inside was a plain room with one little window,

a desk and a wardrobe.

'I wonder what's in here,' said Damon, with the same look in his eyes that he'd had when he pulled the louvre out. He yanked at the wardrobe door.

I stood in the middle of the room willing him to stop, but knowing he wouldn't. I prayed no one would come.

When the wardrobe wouldn't open he moved to the desk. On top of it was a Children's Edition Bible, a notepad and a pen, and a mug with dregs of old coffee.

'What's the priest like?' he asked.

'I dunno. S'pose he's all right.'

Damon wrote 'dickhead' across the first page of the notepad. 'He'll probably vomit when he sees this,' he said. He looked in the desk drawers. 'This priest's got lots of magazines.' He held up an old *Women's Weekly*.

I heard a noise from outside, a scuffling: it was so quiet I might have imagined it. I wished I hadn't made up the story about the security guard because now I wasn't sure I trusted my ears.

'Woah, look at all this stuff!' Damon held up some cards with gold-painted edges. On one side was a picture of a guardian angel watching over a boy and girl playing near a cliff above a raging river. On the other side was a prayer. He put half of the cards in his pocket. Next he held up a handful of silvery religious medallions with saints on them. He said, 'A shop-keeper might think they're ten centses if we mix 'em in with other money.'

The noise outside seemed to have stopped. Damon scooped the medallions into his shorts pockets with the cricket ball and the cards.

For God's sake stop stealing stuff, is what I was going to say, but before I could he said, 'Hey look,' and from under the desk he produced a bottle. 'Wine.' He twisted the top but it wouldn't open.

'Let's take it! We can drink it later,' I said, all the while thinking, *What the hell are you saying?* and also *Now he can't say you're a chicken*, and *Maybe now he'll stop and we can get the hell out of here.*

'Way ahead of you,' he said and he put it under his shirt. Already I'd changed my mind. *No, let's leave it*, was what I wanted to say, but the words wouldn't come. I edged the door open to check that the church was still empty.

It wasn't. Far back among the pews was an old woman in a blue cardigan, her head bowed. She wasn't moving. Was she sleeping? Praying?

'Is there another way out?' whispered Damon.

I shook my head.

We waited. Eventually Damon said in a low voice, 'Gunna have to go for it,' and he began tiptoeing past the altar. I followed, my eyes staying on the old lady all the way to the door.

Outside, we ran, leaving the church behind us like a gigantic iceberg. I almost cried with relief to be in daylight with the birds and the wind rustling the branches of the trees.

'Did she see us?'

'Nup,' said Damon with no echo now. 'Bet that's the first time you've flogged something.'

'Yep. I couldn't do that again.'

'Why not? You did okay.'

It felt like the highest compliment I'd ever got. And I thought to myself, *There's no way anyone's going to walk down this lane right now. Fifty steps and we're free.* And then I thought, *Who's the worst person that could turn up? A policeman? Mum? The priest?*

And then Father Lockhart appeared round the corner. He walked up to us, smiling a friendly smile, his face all cheeks, bald but for a few strands of comb-over. 'Afternoon, boys,' he said. Then he stood hands in pockets, rocking on his heels, waiting for a reply.

I said, 'Afternoon, Father.'

Oh God, please don't let him recognise me.

I glanced at Damon, who had his hands behind his back.

'What are you boys up to this fine day?' said Father Lockhart with a laugh in his voice—he always seemed to find anything a kid said or did funny.

'Just playing,' said Damon and, fishing in his pocket, he produced the cricket ball and held it up as proof.

'Six stitcher, ay? Can I see it?' asked Father Lockhart.

Damon chucked it to him and Father caught it. He put it to the light and examined its stitches.

'Can you spin it?' he asked.

'What?' said Damon.

'Can you bowl spin? You know, cricket.'

'Oh. Nup.'

Father Lockhart threw the ball up, flicking his wrist as he did, and the ball spun crazily. Then when it hit the ground it bounced almost sideways and he stopped it awkwardly with his foot. He bent to pick it up.

'You have to put your fingers like this. See? I couldn't do it either, but I practised every day then after a while it was easy. Perseverance is the thing, as in everything in life,' he said, and he chucked the ball back to Damon. 'You practise and soon you'll be taking more wickets than you can poke a stick at. Anyway, on you go, boys.'

'See you, Father' I replied.

He started whistling as he kept on towards the church, and we kept on up the lane.

'Is he gone?' asked Damon without looking back.

I looked round. He was gone.

'What did you do with the wine?' I asked.

Instead of answering, he ran back, his pockets jangling with the medallions. He stuck his head into the hedge, then returned with the bottle.

'Let's take it back,' I whispered.

Damon looked over his shoulder. 'I think he went into the church. We can't.' He put the bottle under his shirt and we ran back through the school grounds, back across the oval, back along Shoe Street, with me thinking, *That was robbery. Did we really just do that? Did I do that?*

But there was Damon beside me with the bottle: we'd done it all right. I was a robber. If Father had been a minute earlier we'd have been caught.

'That was close,' said Damon. 'Fun though.'

'You think it's fun to be nearly caught stealing?' It was an actual question, but he laughed. I was laughing too, but also thinking, *Why am I laughing? What's wrong with me?*

'Where should we hide it?' asked Damon.

'The swamp?' It was the first place that popped into my head.

'Good one,' said Damon, 'Lucky Connor wasn't here. He would've had pee all down his leg.'

I laughed again. I wished Connor had heard *that*.

We made our way along the track. By then it was about two and the sun was at its hottest and everything was slow and beaten down except one little bird that buzzed above and below the grass like a stone skipping on smooth water.

At the clearing Damon hid the bottle in the reeds and stood back, checking the spot from different angles. No, he didn't like it there. He retrieved it, wiped the mud off, and slid it up the drainpipe that protruded from the bank.

'I can't see that. Can you see it?' he said.

The drainpipe was big enough to crawl into—the thought made me shudder. I looked up it and couldn't see anything except blackness.

Damon dug a handful of medallions out of his pocket and put them with the wine, and then he put some prayer cards up there as well. 'I got something else too,' he said and he held out a closed fist. He opened it slowly, watching my reaction.

It was a string of rosary beads. Each bead was gold.

Each chain link was gold. The crucifix was glinting gold, and there was a red stone above Jesus' head that didn't look like plastic. Old, obviously, and valuable. Like something in a museum.

'It was in the drawer. Be worth about five hundred dollars, I reckon. Think I'll sell it on the black market.'

I pictured pirates in a smoky bar with piles of gold coins on the table.

'You can have half,' he said. He was still watching my face, daring me to say he shouldn't have taken them, *expecting* me to say it, getting ready to pounce on me when I did.

I shrugged casually, carelessly.

He said, 'I do stuff like this all the time.' Then he reached into the drainpipe and dropped the beads there with the other things.

'The priest probably won't even notice they're gone. You know you can't say anything about this to anyone, right?'

'I won't.'

'Not even Connor. You've gotta swear.'

'I swear.'

'Put your hand like this,' he said, and he shaped my hand into a salute like the cub salute. 'Say: "I swear on my mother's grave I will never tell anyone about what we did today.'"

I said it.

He gave me one of the prayer cards. 'This can be your share for now. Go home. I'll see you round. And remember—*no one.*'

I walked back along Shoe Street with the prayer card in my pocket. We'd done a terrible thing, I knew, an unforgiveable thing, a life-changingly earth-shatteringly awful thing. And a stupid thing—we'd be caught for sure. It seemed to me a bottle of wine might not be missed, but a gold rosary—Father would *definitely* notice *that* was gone. And he'd *seen* us.

I stopped in my tracks as that sank in.

I felt like throwing myself on the ground. Instead, I ran. Thankfully no one was on the street. Anyone who saw my face would've gone straight and called the police: '*Don't know what this kid's done but it's something bad. Murder, probably.*'

At home I hurried to my room and put the card in my undies drawer. Then I went into the lounge room and turned on the TV and watched *Star Blazers* and then *Six of the Best* and then *Neighbours* and then the news without taking my eyes off the TV as outside the sun went down and night set in.

3
THE END OF THE UNIVERSE

'YOU STUPID IDIOT!' said Darth Vader. 'I can't believe you just did that. You fool.' He was yelling at a storm-trooper who'd dropped the Crystal of Doom.

'Get him! Kill him!' said Luke to Han Solo. They were trying to rescue the Crystal of Doom before it went into meltdown. 'Han, you idiot. What are you doing?' Luke was on edge because Han kept shooting his laser near the crystal despite knowing it contained enough nuclear power to explode the whole universe.

I was on my bedroom floor producing/directing an epic *Star Wars* game, which also involved some dinosaurs and a few GI Joes. I was too old to play *Star Wars*; Connor called me a nutjob. But it took my mind off things when I was stressed.

The stormtrooper dropped the Crystal of Doom

again. Darth Vader choked him to death. Then Han Solo fired his laser one last time.

'*Noooo*,' yelled Luke.

'*Noooo*,' bellowed Darth Vader.

Kbooooom!

It was the biggest explosion ever. Lego was flying everywhere. A tyrannosaurus was blasted so high it hit the roof. Darth Vader and Han Solo and Luke Skywalker sailed across the room and into the wall.

I sat back, stunned. 'You know what this means?' I said in Luke's voice, though of course it wasn't Luke talking: he was dead. Everyone was dead. The universe—the *entire* universe—had exploded. Just like that.

Nothing was left but silence. And then into that silence came a purring, sinister voice: '*Aren't you the kid that stole the rosary beads from the church?*'

It was my conscience. Mostly my conscience sounded high-pitched and annoying, kind of like my own voice, but not always. The time I killed the goldfish it had sounded deep and ominous like Darth Vader. This time it sounded even deeper than that. Like a black panther, twice as big as me, or maybe four times as big. I imagined it sitting on my bedroom floor licking its paw with a what's-it-to-you? attitude.

My conscience-panther stood up, stalked around the room, then stopped in front of my cupboard, which was half hang-up section and half drawers, and nuzzled my undies drawer. '*What's in here, I wonder. Something stolen, perhaps?*' it said, like it thought I'd forgotten.

Mum hadn't hassled me about breakfast, it being both a Saturday and the school holidays. I got back into bed with the intention of staying there all day. I took Darth Vader and a dinosaur with me but couldn't get another game going. It didn't help that Boba Fett, my favourite, was missing. If Oliver West hadn't been in Ingham I could have told him about the universe exploding, which struck me as a weird occurrence because *I* was supposed to be in charge of the game but I totally hadn't seen it coming. Probably it meant something, like dreams mean things: *the universe ended in your* Star Wars *game? That means great change is coming*, or, *You're going to travel*, or, *You're totally screwed.*

I could fake that I was sick. I'd done that before, to get out of school.

I was the kind of kid who felt guilty a lot; for instance, I could work up a fair guilt just eating the last chip. But this was different. This guilty was big and

27

black and purring and was starting to look hungry.

I was getting hungry too, so I crept out to the kitchen, with my conscience-panther padding along behind me.

Connor had left his breakfast bowl on the kitchen table and the milk sweating on the sideboard. The clock radio said quarter past ten. The phone was off the hook, which meant Mum was sleeping in; I put it back on its hook and then had some Weetbix. I wondered whether Damon was feeling guilty, and decided that he probably wasn't.

I went downstairs and listened at Connor's bedroom door with my ear pressed against the 'Connor's Room—Keep Out' sign. Connor and I used to sleep in the same room in bunks, but after Christmas Mum had cleared out the storage room and she and Connor painted it, and now it was his room and I had the bunks to myself. So it was even easier for him to avoid me. I knew he was in there: it was too quiet.

I knocked, gently.

No answer.

'Connor?'

Nothing.

I went back to bed and stared at the empty bunk above me, with the foam bulging through the springs in diamond shapes. My bed creaked: the panther had followed me; had curled up at my feet; was watching me. It glanced at my undies draw. *Yes, I know*, I thought. *What do you want me to do about it?* It looked away as if no longer interested. *Thanks. You're a big help.*

I blinked a few hard blinks. *Okay, Aaron, you've stolen some rosary beads from a priest. What now?* I'd dug a hole for myself so deep it had bats and stalagmites and stalactites and ponds with fish that didn't have eyes, but I was bloody well going to find myself a way out of it.

After half an hour of thinking, the only 'way out' I'd come up with was to hope no one would notice anything was missing and that it would all blow over.

Mum was up. I could hear her banging around in the kitchen.

After a while she called out, 'Lunch is ready.'

I took a deep breath and got out of bed.

Mum was at the sink and Connor was at the kitchen table with a book in front of his face when I strolled in.

'Good morning' I said, trying to sound breezy, but it came out like I was an alien in disguise and *good morning* were the first words I'd ever spoken.

'Morning,' said Mum. She was in her pub uniform. She smelled of cigarettes, even though she was supposed to have given up.

She'd made ham sandwiches for us and cheese and lettuce sandwiches for herself—she was trialling vegetarianism. She said, 'Don't think I'm doing this every day. You're old enough to make yourselves a sandwich. I'm gunna be working a lot this week, and when I'm not here I don't want you to just watch TV. Why don't you play with your Monopoly game, Aaron?'

I shrugged. She'd got it from Vinnies. The lid was sticky-taped together and some of the cards were missing. And, anyway, it required at least one other person to play *against*.

'Where've you been?' I asked Connor.

He finished chewing. 'None of your biz.'

'Yeah, where've you been?' said Mum from behind her little make-up mirror.

Connor sighed. 'I was in my room, of course. Reading.'

Mum pulled her hair into a ponytail. 'Well, I want you two to play together this arvo,' she said as she picked up her bag and rushed down the front stairs.

As soon as she was gone Connor skulked off to his room and I was by myself again. So far so good.

Later, I was watching TV when I heard a motorbike revving up the driveway, which meant Mum had finished work early and hitched a lift back with Bernie.

After a while I went into the kitchen to tell Mum that I wasn't feeling very well so it wouldn't look so weird if I spent all day inside. Bernie was at his spot at the table next to the louvre windows and Mum was reading a magazine. They were both drinking beer.

'Here's Aaron,' said Mum.

'Here's the big fella,' said Bernie. 'High school this year, ay? How's your holidays going?'

'Okay,' I said. 'Mum, I don't feel very well.'

'Have some cough syrup,' she replied and then she turned to Bernie. 'You know, they haven't done a thing all holidays except sit around and watch TV. I should send them round to the old people's home or something. Or get them to do some chores around here.'

I got the cough syrup bottle from the cupboard and poured myself a medicine cup of the sweet dark red syrup, then sat at the table and sipped it while they talked.

'My holidays I used to work on me neighbours' farm. Got two bucks an hour,' said Bernie, and Mum said, 'I'm too much of a softie.'

Bernie shook his head, smirked in a they've-got-it-easy way and took a sip of beer. Bernie usually came round on Fridays after work, stomped up our back stairs, put a six-pack of beer in the fridge and his feet up on one of our kitchen chairs. And he stayed like that till Mum shooed him out around dinner time. His hair was curly and his beard neatly trimmed, and he was so big he made Mum and Connor and me look like midgets.

He said, 'Had a good arvo at Gary's. You should've come, Trace. You missed out.'

Mum pulled a face. 'I've got no desire to sit around watching them get pissed. I like Heather, but Gary gives me the shits with all his carry-on. Time he grew up, I reckon.'

'So you were at Pete's place, were ya?' Bernie said slyly. 'You know he goes down the RSL with Mungo and them.'

'Who's Pete?' I asked Mum, but she just said, 'A friend,' and shook her head at Bernie, who changed the subject by saying, 'You know Fay's leaving on Tuesday.'

They gossiped a bit about Fay. Then Bernie finished his beer, stood up, stretched and gave Mum a hug (which was unusual). Then he shook my hand and went downstairs, and we heard his Harley rev out through the gate.

After Bernie left, Mum threw down her magazine

and said, 'I'm sick of getting a lift all the time. Go get Connor and we'll go to Gran's and borrow the car.'

I coughed. 'Can I stay home?' I said. 'The cough syrup didn't do anything.'

She glanced at me over her shoulder. 'You're fine. Get your shoes on.'

Gran's house was three blocks away. You could walk to most places in Fingleton, the crappest town in Far North Queensland, a part of Australia no one ever thought about except when the occasional cyclone came and blew everything to bits. It was built on a river only one turn from the sea, and it had a bunch of butchers and bakers and pubs, plus a picture theatre (at which I'd seen *ET*, *The Empire Strikes Back* and *Annie*) and a shop that sold crystals and dreamcatchers and incense, and, further out, a scout hut and a BMX track. Fingleton didn't have traffic lights or a McDonalds. Around it was mostly sugarcane and banana farms, and rainforest-covered mountains. A hundred years ago it'd all been rainforest but the farmers had cut most of it down, except for one or two forgotten patches.

I followed Mum and Connor along the footpath, my head down. I felt like people were watching me from every window. Flat, dried toads dotted the road.

33

The sun bore down on us. There was no breeze—if you didn't count the panther's breath on my neck as it followed close behind me.

Gran's house was on stilts like ours, but she had pink flamingos in her front yard and a pink bougainvillea whose thorns attacked your face and arms as you walked up her front stairs.

Gran answered the door in her dirty-at-the-knees garden pants, a T-shirt and her puppy-dog slippers. She was sweat-free: she said she was immune to the heat because she'd lived in the Far North all her life—before there were fans, even.

She said, 'It feels like a lifetime since I saw you boys,' and she kissed Connor on his sweaty forehead but did an air kiss for me.

Obviously I didn't *want* a kiss, but it seemed odd.

'We can't stay, Gran,' said Mum. 'I was wondering if we could borrow the Mini. I want to look at some houses.'

But Gran had got behind us and she was sweeping us in, saying, 'I'll get you a cuppa and the boys can have a bikkie.'

Sunlight sweltered through the the curtains in her lounge room and shone off her Elvis Presley paintings, which she'd done herself. Gran had judged three

Elvis-lookalike competitions, and even though she was thin and stooped she still did rock-n-roll dancing every Sunday afternoon with the Elvis Dancers.

She led us to the kitchen, which thankfully had louvres and so there was a breeze, and she sat us at the table with a plate of Anzac biscuits. The radio was on the local station with DJ Mike the Mike, who played lots of Elvis. Mum hated him.

Mum let Gran pour her a tea.

'Your father got your letters,' said Gran.

My dad left when I was five and I hadn't seen him since. He never called us. Sometimes he wrote letters that Gran gave us, and she got us to write replies, which she sent to him. That's just the way it was.

'He's in Mount Isa at the moment,' said Gran, then caught herself, like she hadn't meant to say it. She glanced at Mum.

'That's not that far is it?' I asked, to say something, so Connor wouldn't say, *Hey, Aaron, you're being quiet.*

'It's like a day's drive,' said Connor.

'Anyway, he loved the letters and asked me to give you these,' said Gran, and she handed us each a double-ended pencil. Connor got blue and red; I got green and yellow.

Mum bit her lip—she hated Dad's presents.

Gran said, 'You can use them to draw your Dad a picture, and we can post them with the next letters. Why don't you send the boys round with them when they're finished, Trace?'

'Sure, Gran, I'll send them round,' said Mum. She was gulping her tea.

'Now,' said Gran, 'Did I ever tell you boys about the time your dad played in the schoolboys' final?'

Gran had an unspoken rule—if we wanted the car we had to listen to a story.

'Your dad was in the first team and he was only in grade ten. I said to the coach, "He's too small," and the coach said—'

'You told us, Gran,' said Connor through a mouthful of Anzac biscuit. Gran looked a bit put out till Mum said, 'Why don't you tell us about the old days when you lived out on the farm? There were Aboriginal people living on the property, weren't there?'

Gran looked thoughtful. 'When my dad was a boy there were. A family lived on the riverbank. They used to catch fish and swap them for bread. They used to leave the fish on the back stairs.'

'Do you know any Dreamtime stories?' I asked.

The Dreamtime was a long time ago when

everything got made; we'd learnt about it at school.

'I do remember a story—about rainfish,' said Gran.

I said, 'I know that one.'

'Now, how did it go?' She sipped her tea. 'A long time ago,' she began, 'in the Dreamtime,' she added, 'a little Aboriginal boy caught a fish, and the fish said, "I am the king of fish, the magical rainfish, and if you let me go, I'll give you three wishes." And so the boy said, "I want a castle all of gold," and *whoosh*, there was a castle, with many towers all of gold, and flags of gold thread, and a moat of liquid gold. And then he said, "I want to be king of all the world," and *whoosh*, a crown appeared on his head so large it was all he could do to keep it from falling off. And then for his last wish the boy said, "I want to be king of all the things there are, including the rivers and the sea and the sky and the stars," and then the rainfish got angry and said, "You greedy boy, now you get nothing," and then the crown and the castle disappeared and he was left with just his own silly self. Let that be a lesson to you boys—don't be too greedy!' she finished with satisfaction.

'Why was the fish called the rainfish?' asked Connor.

'*Hmm*,' said Gran. 'It was a while ago I heard that story...'

'That's wrong, Gran,' I said, because I knew the proper rainfish story, but as usual no one paid me any attention.

Mum had taken a finishing slug of her tea and was about to stand up when Gran said, 'And what about that business at the church?'

I bit down hard on my tongue. The panther purred in an I-told-you-so way.

'What business at the church?' said Mum.

'Haven't you seen the paper? Here, have a look.' Gran pulled the *Fingleton Gazette* from her bag, thumbed through it then passed it to Connor, saying, 'Read it out, dear.'

Connor lay the paper on the table and read:

Police Round-up. Church Broken Into

The Saint Rita's Church vestry was broken into on Friday and ransacked. A number of items were stolen, including a string of gold rosary beads. Father Terry Lockhart said the beads had significant sentimental value: they were a gift from his late father. Police have examined the scene. Anyone with information please call Crime Stoppers.

Police have examined the scene!
I shuddered.

'What kind of monster would steal from a church?' said Mum.

I looked down at my hands; they'd gone white.

'The mafia,' said Connor.

'Maureen said Father Lockhart is taking stress leave,' said Gran, 'He's writing to the bishop. But don't say anything to anyone. I don't think he'll be back in time for the Start of Term Mass.'

'It'd be kids,' said Mum. 'Some people let their kids run wild like stray dogs.'

I took another biscuit and chewed at it.

Connor was watching me. He knew, I could tell. He always seemed to know what I was thinking.

Mum stood up. 'Say thank you, boys.'

We said thank you. Gran's smile seemed to tighten when she swung it in my direction, and again I missed out on a kiss. *What was going on?*

We rushed down the back stairs to Gran's Mini, doors thumping, engine revving, and finally we had the car back. I'd missed the car smell, the grainy radio, the straining at the seatbelt to hear Mum and Connor's front-seat conversation. But with the story in the paper churning in my mind, this time I was only half-listening.

'Mount Isa's about a day's drive away, right?' said Connor.

We were idling in front of a house for sale, a red brick one with a trampoline in the front yard.

'Mount bloody Isa,' said Mum, 'is in the middle of the bloody country. You drive about fourteen hours on the straightest, most boring road in the world, no towns or trees or anything—just desert. And if your car breaks down you're dead: only a few cars come along every week. And *if* you survive the drive you get to a crappy town with a big factory in the middle spewing poison all over everyone giving them cancer *and* brain damage.' After a bit she added, 'Anyway, he might not be there. Then you'd look silly, wandering around Mount Isa saying, "Isn't this nice."'

'Yeah, all right, I get it,' said Connor.

We bought fish and chips, and then drove with them to the beach at the river mouth and sat on the sand and ate them, and we watched the water roll out with the tide and the sun sink in a sky of pink and purple.

Mum began in an offhand way. 'You know Peter? My friend that I've mentioned?'

It was getting darker and I couldn't see her face, only her silhouette. *Peter?* I'd definitely heard the name.

'You mean the one you've mentioned like a hundred times?' said Connor.

'Well, I just thought I'd tell you, actually, that he's a special friend of mine. So I thought it might be a good thing if you two met him. So we're all going out to dinner tomorrow night.'

'Where to?' asked Connor.

'Mario's.'

'What sort of food is that?' I asked.

'It's Italian, you idiot,' said Connor.

'Connor,' sighed Mum.

'But it's like the *most* Italian name there is.'

'That's enough,' said Mum.

We threw the leftover chips into the water. Then in the dark we stumbled up the beach to Gran's Mini, the only car under the single streetlight in the sandy carpark.

Back at home we watched *The A-Team*, but I wasn't paying attention. I'd just remembered that Gran had a blue cardigan just like the one the lady in the church was wearing when we'd taken the rosary beads. The black panther, next to me on the couch, sniggered and shook its head: '*Great job, Aaron. Terrific. So smart. You're going down, mate. You're going down.*

4

DETECTIVE CONNOR

THE MORNING AFTER we'd been to Gran's I crept
to the kitchen with the intention of slamming down
my breakfast and then skulking back to my room. But
there Connor was at the table drinking coffee. (He had
it white with three sugars, and he didn't particularly
like it, in my opinion, but he thought it made him look
grown-up.) 'Aaron,' he said. 'Just the man. Get some
Weetbix and take a chair.'

When I sat down he said, 'You know that church
thing?'

'Ummm,' I said, trying to sound as if I wasn't sure.

'Someone broke into the church. Remember?'

'Oh yeah, that's right.'

He looked at me like I couldn't have been a bigger
idiot even if I'd been wearing a helmet made from a

watermelon. 'That's right,' he said. 'I don't reckon it was the mafia anymore.'

I took a nonchalant spoonful of Weetbix, swallowed it, and said, 'So who do you think it was?'

'I've got some ideas. My main one is that it was a kid.'

'I don't think so,' I said.

He raised his eyebrows. 'How would *you* know?'

I shrugged. 'Just don't reckon it was a kid, that's all.' I thought about it some more and then I said, 'Kids don't do that sort of stuff.'

'That's primary-school thinking, Aaron. You've got to get out of that.' He took a sip of coffee. 'See, in detective work you can't just rule out a whole group of people like that. You've got to be scientific. When you start a case everyone's a suspect. Like in "Guess Who". You've played that, right?' He didn't wait for an answer. 'You use *evidence* to rule people out, and then the last person not ruled out is the killer, or the thief, or whatever. I read a book about detectives a few weeks ago. Which was good timing, 'cause I've decided to take on the case of the rosary-beads thief.'

I nodded—somehow I'd known he was going to. It was typical of him. And it was also typical that he'd just read a book about detectives. Connor was a lunchtime library kid. He was always reading, the bigger the book the better. He'd read more than his teacher, who he hated because she'd given him a B for one of his stories. He could even read Elvish, and sometimes he wrote in his diary in a mixture of Elvish Runes and Egyptian hieroglyphics.

Connor and I had the same hair and we both had freckles (not freckles like Damon's: ours weren't orange splotches, they were small dark-brown dots). But Connor was taller than me, and he wore reading glasses, but *only* when he was reading; he was self-conscious about them.

He was skinny. Mum said he'd been skinny ever since he was a baby. He'd been born blue, and after that he was in a humidicrib for a long time. He had asthma, and sometimes when he had an attack we'd all go up to the hospital. Usually Sister Osgood would be on in Emergency—she's Mum's friend—and she'd say, 'Have you come to stay in your holiday room again, Connor?' Actually it was just a normal kids' hospital room, with a cardboard plane mobile hanging from the ceiling, a greying beanbag on the floor and a Connect Four set with half the pieces missing.

Once Connor'd had to go by ambulance to intensive care in a bigger hospital. Having asthma meant he got loads of sympathy and he had an excuse for not being good at sport, whereas I had no excuses. For brothers we really didn't have much in common.

'First thing I'm going to do is make a list of suspects. There's a detective who solves all his cases without getting out of bed, just by using deduction. His butler gets the evidence for him. If I need you to get anything for me I'll call out,' he said and he went back down to his room.

I spent the morning in front of the TV worrying about how Connor's investigation was getting on. Connor had the kind of weird mind that sometimes saw things before other people, though at other times he'd miss things that were right in front of his face. I wouldn't be surprised if he worked out it was me. When I turned the TV off, the face I saw reflected in the dark screen looked like it was straight from a 'wanted for murder' poster.

When Connor came out to the kitchen at lunchtime I was waiting for him. 'Did you solve it?' I asked.

'Not yet.' He got the peanut butter from the cupboard and the bread from the freezer and started making a sandwich. 'I've made a list of suspects,' he said. 'But I think I need to go check out the scene of the crime. You can come if you want.'

'Nah.'

'Suit yourself.'

I watched from the front veranda as he set off along our street, with his schoolbag on his back. Why did he need his bag? I wondered. Did he have his magnifying glass in it (the one from his stamp collector's kit)? Some rope to tie the thief up with? A muesli bar? Did he take the list of suspects with him? I wondered. Probably he took it. But maybe he didn't. Maybe he left it in his room. It was worth a look. I raced down the back stairs.

Something was different about the 'Connor's Room—Keep Out' sign. There it was: he'd added 'Aaron' after 'Keep Out'. Like that was going to do anything.

Even though I'd just seen him leave, out of habit, or maybe superstition, I knocked. Then I gently pushed the door open.

Inside, it was dark, and musty from the pile of towels and dirty clothes next to his bed. There was a *Star Wars* poster on the wall and luminous stars stuck on the black-painted ceiling. On his desk was his old homework book, open. I was careful not to touch it so I wouldn't leave any fingerprints. The page was divided into two columns, labelled 'Possibles' and 'Probables'. Under 'Probables', from top to bottom, was: Stevie Harmison, state school kids, Mafia, devil worshippers, criminal gangs. The entries under 'Possibles' filled the column, and some were written sideways in the margin. I was shocked to see my name was there, but then I felt a bit better to see Connor's was there too, though that had been crossed out. Also making the list was 'Priest (inside job)', and 'Mrs Melchiori's son', and some names I didn't recognise, and almost every kid in Connor's class. Damon's name was there too.

I ran back upstairs and tried to control my breathing to make it look like I hadn't moved from in front of the TV, but I needn't have bothered, because the first person home was Mum, and that wasn't till about half-past four. At six Connor still wasn't back, and Mum and I had had our showers and were ready to go to Mario's. Mum had her red dress on and her hair tied back, and make-up on, which made her look angrier than normal.

'You're not wearing that! Go and put your button-up shirt on,' said Mum, but before I could she asked me again, 'Did he say where he was going?'

'No, he didn't say.'

I put my button-up shirt on—it had little ice-creams

all over it—then took the prayer card out of my undies drawer and put it in my shorts pocket. I immediately felt calmer. The undies drawer was such an obvious hiding place for Connor to look; I'd have to think of somewhere else.

By the time Connor came trudging up the back stairs like a returning explorer we were late and Mum wasn't happy. 'Where the hell have you been? Come on, you haven't got time for a shower. Just put your good clothes on and get in the bloody car.'

Connor got ready and we drove in the Mini to Edith Street, to 'Mario's Italian Restaurant', as the sign said in red and green on a white background, with red-and-white-checked plastic tablecloths and cane chairs. And there was Peter, sitting at a table for four by the window, looking out at the street. When he saw us he stood up.

He was a tall man with tattoos on his arms. The tattoos were the first things I noticed. Especially the dolphin on his hairy forearm, in two shades of blue, and a crude anchor that looked like a dot-to-dot picture on his wrist.

He had a short red beard and big ears that stuck out like mug handles. His hair was receding, and he had freckles like a boy's. His checked shirt looked new and out of place against the sunburnt skin and tattoos of his arms.

I'd pictured someone like the photos I'd seen of Dad, or maybe a bikie in a leather jacket, but he wasn't like that. He looked more like a pirate who'd just taken off his eye patch and shooed away his parrot.

'Hey, Peter,' said Mum. 'Been waiting long?'

'Nup. Not at all,' he said.

'Connor, Aaron, this is Peter.'

'Hello, men,' Peter said in a gruff jokey voice.

He shook hands with me like I was a businessman, squeezing my hand so tightly that it hurt, though I'm sure he didn't mean it to.

When we looked at the menu he snorted and said, 'No steak and chips!'

We all smiled.

Mum got gnocchi, Connor got lasagne, I got lasagne, and Peter got lasagne too.

'Where'd you go?' I whispered to Connor while we waited for our food.

'All over the place. I even went into town.'

'Find anything?'

'Found a clue.'

'What clue?'

'That's for me to know and you to find out,' he said

with a little smile that I didn't like one bit.

Peter turned to Mum. 'Might be goin' up to Malanda in the morning.'

'Peter drives a truck,' said Mum to Connor and me.

Connor stopped playing with his knife and fork. 'What sort of truck?' he said.

'It's a little Ford,' said Peter.

'How many wheels does it have?'

'Geez, let me think. Eight, how's that?'

Connor snorted, 'Some trucks have way more than that.'

'Yep, that's true,' agreed Peter, and he had a sip of his beer. 'Have you ever tasted beer?' he asked Connor.

'We're not allowed.'

'One taste won't kill anyone!'

'Can we, Mum, please?' I said.

'All right. Just this once. And just a sip.'

Both of us had a sip, Connor first.

'Yuck!' I said, and Peter laughed loudly.

'It's not all that bad,' said Connor.

'Peter used to be a sea captain,' said Mum.

'What sort of ship was it?' asked Connor.

'A prawn trawler,' said Peter.

'Peter's a famous barra fisherman. One of the best in town, aren't you, Peter?' Mum gave him a wry smile.

'That's what I've heard, anyway.'

'Come off it!' said Peter, but he reddened and grinned from ear to ear.

'How come you're the best fisherman?' I asked.

'Well,' he said, and he leaned in.

We all leaned in with him.

'I've got a secret spot,' he whispered. 'Only me and maybe one or two other people know about it.'

'Can we go?'

'Usually when I take people, I blindfold them.'

Connor smiled. 'That's not true.'

Mum said, 'He's serious.'

Peter said, 'I'm serious all right. You can't have everyone blabbing about it—there'd be no fish left.'

'What's so good about fishing?' said Connor, meaning that he didn't like it.

But Peter took it as a serious question and so he attempted an answer. 'What's so good about fishing? Let's see. You get to breathe some fresh air for one thing.' He took a drink, smacked his lips, put his beer down. 'Tell you what—instead of me just saying it, how 'bout I tell you a fishing story?'

'Do it, Peter,' said Mum, and Peter said, 'All right,' and he settled back in his chair. 'Now this happened to a mate of mine not long back. One day, he goes out in his tinny up the river to Sandfly Creek to check his crab pots. You been to Sandfly Creek?'

We hadn't, but I'd heard friends talking about it. It was in the swampy part of the river just near the mouth, where mangroves crowded the banks and egrets made their nests on branches that hung over the water.

'Well, it's a bendy little mangrove creek, and the water's always murky so you can't see how deep it is. It's kind of a dark, kind of a creepy, crawly sort of place. Anyway, my mate anchors right in the mangroves, then drops a handline with a prawn on it over the side. Then he sits down and starts havin' his lunch. Next thing he sees the line move so he picks it up and he feels a little bite: nibble, nibble.' This bit he whispered. 'Then nothing. Then nibble, nibble, nibble. Then nothing. Then bang!'

He said that loud enough to make the waiter and the people next to us turn around.

'At first it was just a steady pull, so he pulled back. Then it ran, full bore. He sees something's just under the surface upstream making a bow wave, something really big just under the water, but because it's so murky he can't really see what it is. Anyway, he starts his motor up to follow it. He doesn't want to play it too much in those mangrove roots because he'll get a snag and lose it. So he's following the bow wave, going upstream and he still can't see what it is. Then, just when he's getting closer, the thing turns and goes up a big drainpipe that's feeding into the creek. Inside there it's dark like a cave. You can't get a boat up in something like that, so he can't do anything, just puts some pressure on the line. But it's not stopping, it just keeps goin' and goin' and eventually—bang! Snaps the line. And that's the story.'

And Peter sat back, looking pleased with himself.

Connor said, 'So what was it?'

Peter's beady eyes sparkled. 'Croc? Something else? Who knows? Me mate could've gone up the drain if he really wanted to know. Anyway, that's the point. That's the thing about fishing. Whenever you chuck your line in and something bites, till you get it up flappin' in the boat, it could be anything.'

I said, 'Tell us another one.'

But Mum put her arm out as if to hold him back, and said to me, 'Let him have a rest, Aaron.'

After dinner we all got dessert. Peter and Mum were both giggly. Mum had moved her chair closer to his so their arms were touching, like she was a schoolgirl, though she was probably older than him. She laughed at some dumb joke he made, and let her head fall to rest on his shoulder.

When the bill came, Peter said, 'Don't worry about it, Tracey, I'll pay for everything,' and he grandly placed four twenties on the little plate.

We left without getting the change. And Peter shook my hand again when we said goodbye, this time not as tight as the first one.

Before we went to bed Mum made us hot chocolate. We sat at the kitchen table waiting for it to cool.

'You don't make much money being a truck driver, do you,' said Connor.

'I think he does all right,' said Mum. 'And he knows a lot about cars. He's going to help me buy one. I think he's nice.'

I said, 'I hope he takes us fishing to his secret spot.'

'He might,' said Mum, 'if you're good. You never know.'

5

THE CLUE

ON MONDAY MORNING I was under the house in the driver's seat of our Datsun. The left front wheel was buckled and you couldn't open the left front door, because Mum had rammed it into a pole. By accident of course. On school holidays we used to drive to the beach or to Polly's Creek, which was in the rainforest and had a tree you could jump off into the water. You could catch fish and turtles there too. But the poor old Datsun wasn't going to see Polly's Creek again.

The panther was on the back seat watching me, which was a bit of a surprise. I'd kind of assumed he'd wandered off somewhere, but there he was. *'The police are going to catch you,'* it purred. *'And today's Monday and you know what that means.'* What that meant was that the *Fingleton Gazette* was coming out.

The *Fingleton Gazette* came out on Mondays, Wednesdays and Saturdays. The Monday and Wednesday papers were usually only twelve pages of stories about sugarcane and pawpaw and banana prices, and how bad the flying foxes were, and ads for used sugarcane harvesters, and one measly *Phantom* strip, and on the back page stories about Fingleton's hopeless league and cricket and soccer teams. And the Police Round-up with headlines like: 'Garden Gnome Stolen', 'Man Drunk and Disorderly', and 'Windows Broken in Vandalism Spree'.

Mum usually brought the paper home from the pub where she worked, which meant I had all morning before I'd find out if there was anything in it about you-know-what.

A sudden panic hit me. Where was the prayer card? I checked my pockets. It wasn't there. Then I remembered—I ran upstairs and got it out of yesterday's shorts where they lay crumpled on the floor. I hadn't noticed the guardian angel's face before: her smile was kind of frozen as she watched the boy and girl playing. Did she even care whether or not they fell off the cliff?

I couldn't think where to hide it, so I transferred it to the pocket of my new shorts, and then I took yesterday's clothes and put them in the laundry basket in the bathroom. The black panther's hot cat breath was on my neck all the while. Why was it a black panther? Maybe because it was my favourite animal, if anyone ever asked. The name was cool, and I liked a picture I'd seen of one: it was jet black like a hole in the world with a pair of eyes peering out. If I had one as a pet I'd take it to school, and if anyone annoyed me I'd whisper in its ear and *grrrcrack!*—that's the sound of the annoying person's spine breaking. And *chew, slurp*—that's the panther eating their limp remains.

While I ate breakfast that morning the rosary beads incident was forced to the back of my mind by another huge event. In school holidays either nothing happens or everything happens in a bunch, and I was in the middle of the king of all bunches because the new huge event wasn't just any huge event: it was a bombshell explosion, an earth-shatteringly momentous huge event. But this isn't the best time to get into it.

Anyway, after the huge event happened Mum went to work for an hour, then at lunchtime she came back, without the paper, and made us sandwiches. Then she picked up Gran's car keys and her bag again.

'Are you going back to work?' asked Connor, who'd been out most of the morning 'sleuthing', as he put it. I was beginning to hate the snaky sound of that word.

'Nup. I'm going into town to get some spaghetti and maybe some ice cream if you boys are good.'

'Can you *please* get the paper this time?' said Connor.

'What do you want the paper for?'

'I'm investigating the break-in at the church.'

'Are you, just?' she said, in a tone I didn't think he'd like. It was kind of condescending, but Connor didn't seem to notice.

'Yep. And I've found a clue too!'

'Really?' said Mum. 'What's the clue?'

'It's too early in my investigation to make that information public.'

She said, 'Okay, well, I respect that. I'll just have to see if I can live with not knowing.'

When she'd gone he looked at me smugly. 'I know you want to know what the clue is.'

I said, 'Not really,' just to annoy him, and I went and watched TV. I had to turn it up because by that time the huge event was making lots of noise scraping rotten leaves out of our gutter.

I was back in the kitchen when Mum came home. She plonked the paper in front of Connor and said, 'You might want to look at the Police Round-up.'

He snatched it up and turned to the middle pages

and read, then reread whatever it was very slowly. Then he closed it, very, very slowly. 'Interesting,' he said.

'What? Can I have a look?' I asked.

He tossed me the paper and I turned to the Police Round-up column, with its cartoon policeman in sunglasses blowing a whistle at the top.

There were four stories: 'Local Man Arrested Driving while Twice the Legal Limit', 'Service Station Toilet Door Damaged', 'Gunshot Heard on Number Three Branch Road', which was probably some farmboy shooting pigeons with an air rifle, and:

Church Broken Into, Two Boys Seen

On Saturday it was reported that St Rita's Catholic Church had been broken into and a number of items had been stolen, including a valuable string of rosary beads. Police wish to speak to two boys aged about twelve who were seen in the area on Friday. If you have any information regarding this or any other crimes please call Crime Stoppers on...

'Kids don't do that sort of stuff,' said Connor in a moronic voice that was meant to be me. 'You'd make a great detective, Aaron.'

'Might not be them,' I said.

'Yeah, whatever,' said Connor as he made his way down the back stairs.

Mum was still reading her magazine, and the huge event was still outside cleaning the gutters. More than anything I wanted to follow Connor and ask what clue he'd found. To distract myself I went back to watching TV, but there was less than nothing on. I walked twice around the house, including along the weedy side between our house and Joe and Wilma's place, the side we never went down, and under the kitchen window I found a fork, and under Mum's window I found Boba Fett. That was weird, but then I remembered that he'd fallen off Mum's windowsill while fighting Chewbacca and C3PO in the Time Wars back before the universe was destroyed, which seemed like an age ago.

I knocked on Connor's door but he didn't answer, so I ended up kicking the soccer ball round the back-yard by myself. After a while I decided to play out the Intergalactic Soccer Finals, which was something I did a lot—I had the teams and all the players in my mind. Earth was playing Mars that day. I was every player on both teams, but I was especially Aaron Aaronson (rather than Aaron Tate, which was my real name), captain of Australia in soccer, cricket and rugby league, and the greatest individual athlete of all time.

Apart from the fact you had to play around the clothesline and the avocado tree, our backyard made a pretty good soccer field. One goal was two upturned buckets, the other was two stinkbug-covered orange trees that grew about three metres apart near the back of the yard. The banana trees along the back fence and the old empty chook pen in the corner were out of bounds. And if I got hungry I could pick a mandarin from the trees along the side fence we shared with Mrs Melchiori—half the year they were covered with fruit and on the ground rotten mandarins squelched orange-blue-grey through your toes.

I whistled play on, then under my breath took up the commentary in an American accent I'd learnt from TV: 'Aaronson to Maradona. Maradona runs with it, Gwu Gwu (that was the Martian captain) dives in. And misses! Maradona to Aaronson, Aaronson beats one, beats two. Oh no, Gwu Gwu's got it back. He's tricky this Martian...'

By then I was already sweating. The ball's cracked fake leather scratched my bare feet.

'Intercepted! Earth's got it!'

I charged down the centre of the field.

'Aaronson. Oh my God! What a performance! Surely he'll get Man of the Match for this. He beats one, he beats two, he—'

I shot for goal but kicked it way harder than I meant to and the ball flew off towards the back fence.

I didn't find it in the banana trees. Had I kicked it over the fence? I'd never managed that before. Probably it was behind the chook pen, which meant ball lost. Behind the chook pen was a small rectangle of tall guinea grass full of cane toads and hairless tennis balls. A stunted lemon tree that never had any lemons grew there, and under it was an old concrete bathtub with ankle-deep black water in which a million mozzie wrigglers wriggled. The place had a bad air about it. Connor reckoned someone was buried in there.

Sure enough, the ball was peeking through the grass—it was pretty much exactly two metres from me.

It was primary-school thinking to be scared about part of my own backyard. I started for the ball, but a glance at the lemon tree stopped me: there was a spider on a leaf on the branch closest to me. Watching me. It was bigger than my hand. It was so big its weight was causing the leaf to sag. Long shiny legs, yellow spots on its joints, a long, slim, caramel-coloured abdomen. The lemon tree, which was only just taller than me, reached towards the chook pen, so I would have to go side-on to avoid it. Past the spider. It must have been a bird-eating spider. It certainly looked big enough to eat a bird. It was bending its legs rhythmically, like it was gauging the distance it would have to jump to land on me, setting itself to spring.

Someone said, 'Hey!' and I nearly had a stroke.

There was a head sticking up above the back fence. A kid my age, with big ears. He was chewing. I got the feeling he'd been watching me for a while.

I said, 'You nearly made me crap myself.'

He stopped chewing and said, 'You did crap yourself.'

He wanted me to look around and check, but I just said, 'No I didn't.'

'It's all down your leg.'

'Yeah, good one.'

He seemed to think for a while. 'Fuck off,' he said finally, and then he disappeared.

'No, YOU fuck off,' I yelled, though not so loud that it could be heard by Mum in the kitchen.

He didn't answer.

I declared the ball lost and the Intergalactic Finals officially postponed, and as I went back to the house I thought about the reality-shifting fact that there was a boy my age on the other side of my back fence.

That he'd told me to fuck off didn't bother me; most kids in Fingleton said fuck all the time when adults weren't around. Those who didn't were rich—they drove around in nice cars and ate chocolate biscuits. The kids who did say it were rough and poor—they got in trouble, got dirty. If you pushed them too far you'd get a punch in the ear. Everyone wanted to be the second type of kid, so everyone said fuck, which made it hard to distinguish one type from the other. The clue was the way you said it: you needed a casual punchiness. I used to practise saying it, but I never got it quite right because I was a third type: I was like the posh kids but I was poor. Not many kids wanted to hang around with me—usually only Oliver West or Coldy. Connor was even worse at saying fuck than I was, but he had the excuse of being smart. Smart people almost never said fuck right.

The kid over my back fence said it right. I could get walky-talkies, I thought, and throw one over the fence to him and we could talk to each other. Connor wouldn't even know he existed.

I walked around the house a few times, then walked out the front gate and found myself turning right then right again into Shoe Street of all places. I realised I was going to the swamp. Why I was going I had no idea; all I knew was that I had an overpowering urge to be there and that all of a sudden my heart was pumping fast and I had a cold sweat on my neck.

I'd just passed Coldy's place when I heard him yell, 'Aaron!'

He was in his driveway waving at me. He said, 'Where are you going?'

'Nowhere,' I replied.

'Want to come over and play with my train set?' The famous train set: I'd gone over his place with the promise of a go of the train set before, only to be told it was broken or something. There probably wasn't any train set. On the other hand, that time his mum had given me three mint slices.

'Yeah, all right,' I said. 'But just for a bit.'

Coldy's place had fishing nets piled in the front yard with bits of seaweed stuck in them and a crab's claw, and fishing nets spread out under the mango trees in the backyard. Everything smelled like petrol and fish. Under the house was a pulled-to-bits motorbike that belonged to some brother who was so old he had a beard and a girlfriend.

We went upstairs.

'Ross?' Coldy's mum called from their kitchen.

'Yeah, what?'

He shocked me the way he talked to his mum—when he said stuff like that he'd look at me as if to say, *See what a rebel I am?*

'Have you got a friend with you?' she asked in a too-hopeful way, and she stuck her head round the kitchen door with a friendly smile on her face and a smoke in her hand.

Coldy grabbed my arm and pulled me back downstairs, saying, 'Course I have. We're going to go look at the trains.'

'Remember what your dad said about just looking, okay?' said Coldy's mum.

The train set was in a downstairs spare room which was in exactly the same position as Connor's room at our house, which is what had first made me realise that our house and Coldy's were exactly the same. Mum told me that that was because most of our suburb had been built by the sugar mill for the workers in the old days, and it'd been cheaper to just build the same house over and over.

The train set was on a ping-pong table in the middle of the room, complete with painted papier-mâché mountains, a lake of blue cellophane, a city of Monopoly houses and matchbox skyscrapers. Coldy pressed a button on the remote and the train buzzed round the track.

When I asked if I could have a go he held the remote behind his back. 'Dad said I can show people but only *I'm* allowed to control it.'

After a while there was a knock, and Coldy hid the remote as his mum came backing through the door with two cups of Milo and some cream-cheese sandwiches on a tray.

I said, 'Thanks, Mrs Caulderson,' and Coldy said, 'Thanks, Mum,' and she smiled and backed out of the room and we ate the sandwiches and drank the Milo in silence.

Eventually Coldy let me have a go of the train, hovering nervously as I pushed the little lever to full speed.

I had a few goes and then I said, 'Well, I better be off.'

'You can come over and play with it whenever you want. There's more trains in the box. There's a really new one,' said Coldy.

'Yeah, okay. Sounds good,' I replied.

'And I'm getting some new GI Joes next week. A mate of mine's dad works at the GI Joe factory and he said he can get me however many I want. Even ones they don't sell in Australia. You should come over and play with them.'

'Yeah,' I said as I left, thinking, *I, Aaron Tate, hereby pledge not to play with Coldy again for the entire holidays.*

By then it was late afternoon. The cane beetles had begun to emerge from wherever they spent their days, and as I hurried along Shoe Street they were buzzing all around me, and above me the first flying foxes were heading to the banana fields. By dusk they'd be a black stream across the sky.

It occurred to me that I was returning to the scene of the crime just like they say criminals always do. I raced to the T-intersection, then crossed the vacant lot and began to make my way along the path towards the clearing. I thought about crocodiles. They were probably unlikely. But it would have been full of snakes for sure. *Don't think about snakes*, I told myself. *Or anything. Just keep going.*

It was twilight when I slid down the bank. Cicadas were throbbing in the grass all around me. The inside of the drain seemed even blacker than before, and I thought back to Peter's story about the river thing that his friend had caught and wondered if it had escaped up a drain like that one, or maybe one connected to it.

I closed my eyes and put my arm in and felt around.

I felt a breath of cool air. The cold concrete. And then the bottle. And the rosary beads. I pulled them out. For some reason I was relieved to have them in my hands. The rosary beads were heavier than they looked. The gold shone dully, even in the weak light. Some of the beads were worn smooth. I imagined people praying with them down the years, kneeling in churches, over coffins, by sickbeds. I imagined the red jewel being prised from the wall of a jewel mine, and the wonder in the dirty-faced miner's eyes as he held it with both hands. I imagined the beads being passed from the shaky hand of an old man to his young priest son. And now they were my responsibility.

A TV was on in someone's house not far off. I slid the beads back up into the drain and, as the last of the daylight left, started for home.

As I neared our front gate I noticed something in the gutter—it was one of Mum's necklaces. Red glass beads that she never wore. I picked it up.

'What are you doing?' yelled Connor. He was sitting on the front veranda with his back to the wall so you could hardly see him. 'Put it back and come up here.'

I did what I was told. He had his schoolbag next to him and his homework book with the list of suspects.

'It's bait,' he said. 'I think the thieves live close by. If I see someone taking it, then I'll have my prime suspect.'

I knew better than to question his plan: when Connor got an idea in his head it was impossible to get it out. It was reassuring, in a way. He wouldn't be trying something so dumb if he was close to catching us.

'So what was that clue you were talking about?' I asked.

He didn't answer. He was watching the necklace, which was barely visible now in the darkness.

'You didn't find a clue, did you,' I said.

He put his hand into his pocket and then put something into my hand. It was one of the religious medallions.

'Found it on Shoe Street,' he said. 'Detective work, Aaron, is like a giant game of Guess Who. Everyone in the world is on the board to start off with. You get your clues, you start flipping people down. It was someone from around here. For sure. Two boys. They probably live within a block. And I'm going to find them.'

6

AN OLD STORY

THE BEST TREE to climb in our backyard was the avocado tree—it had hardly any green ants or stink-bugs, and there was a branch where you could sit without needing to hold on, and if you tucked your legs up it was a pretty good hiding spot. The next morning I was up there trying to work out what I'd do if the police came. I'd decided to run to the bush near Polly's Creek and find a little hollow and pull a sheet of corrugated iron over it for a roof and then sneak into town on moonless nights to get stuff like a sleeping bag, fishing line to catch fish on and a Swiss army knife for everything else. Also, I was in the tree to avoid Connor, hoping not to give him any more clues.

And apart from that I was reading a book called

Aboriginal Tales of the Far North by Alistair Clarke, which was a collection of stories an explorer reckoned he'd been told by local Aborigines a long time ago. Clarke Park in town was named after Alistair Clarke even though, according to Mum, his 'exploring' had never actually taken him any further north than Brisbane. On the book's tattered cover was a picture of a snake that was supposed to be the rainbow snake that made all the rivers. I was reading it because the thing in the drain in Peter's fishing story had reminded me of the bunyip in the story on page fifty-two. The story was called *The Rainfish*.

'In the Dreamtime,' the story began, 'the local Aboriginal people lived by the riverbank. They ate wallaby and goanna and they speared fish and cooked it on the fire. They had lots of ceremonies, but of all of them the rain ceremony was the most important. But one rainy season, though the people performed their ceremony, the rains didn't come. The old men sang rain songs around the fires at night, they used rain-making stones, but each morning the sky was clearer and bluer than the one before. The water in the streams dried up and all that was left of the river was one muddy little puddle. The kangaroos went off to look for water, and the snakes and the lizards hid in their homes because it was too hot to go outside. The people were thirsty but when they drank the muddy water they got sick.

'One day the old men of the tribe got together and made a plan. They knew that the rainfish controlled the rain and they knew the waterhole where they lived but no one ever went near it because a bunyip lived there. They decided that someone better go and see the rainfish. A boy named Mullaya asked if he could be the one to go.

'Though Mullaya could be reckless, he was a fast runner and brave boy and the elders agreed. So Mullaya set out the next morning carrying his favourite spear.

'The further from the river he got the drier the land became. The rainforest which was usually very green was all dead and grey and the earth was dusty and the grass was curled up and black like it had been burnt in a fire. He walked across the country, he walked for days until he arrived at the home of the rainfish. He knew he was in the right spot because the forest there was still green. But no birds were singing and no animals were around because they were all afraid of that place. Mullaya tiptoed in there, keeping his spear handy, but there was no sign of the bunyip. Soon he came upon a waterhole that was full of clear water. He crept to the edge to take a drink and that was when he saw the rainfish all huddled together asleep in the middle. He splashed with his hand and shouted, "Wake up, rainfish, it's time for it to rain." He threw a rock into the water, but still they didn't wake up. Mullaya became angry then, and he threw his spear into the water and killed one of the rainfish.

'There was a noise like thunder. The rainfish scattered and hid in the reeds, and Mullaya became afraid and ran away, leaving his spear in the water. And as he ran there was a strong wind and behind the wind came rain.

'When Mullaya returned to his tribe they greeted him like a hero and called him "Mullaya the Rainmaker".

'But the rain kept on and didn't stop and soon there was a flood, and the people had to climb the tallest tree in the land so they wouldn't drown.

'Now the bunyip that lived with the rainfish was the sort that swam about. When the floodwaters rose up he left his waterhole and circled the tree, calling out, "Where's that one they call rainmaker?" The old men became suspicious and demanded Mullaya tell them what he had done. When he confessed that he had killed a rainfish they threw him into the water, and the bunyip ate him up. After that the bunyip was satisfied and swam back to his waterhole and the rain stopped and the water went down and the people climbed off the tree again. But from that day on they were careful never to kill a rainfish.'

I closed the book. Just as I thought, it didn't actually say what the bunyip looked like. The first time I'd read it I'd pictured a skeleton monster, or maybe a spider. I hated spiders. Now it sounded more like a dragon or a dinosaur. Maybe a miniature tyrannosaurus that could swim.

'What are you up to?' said Connor, nearly surprising me right off my branch. He was under the avocado tree, with his cricket bat resting on his shoulder. He practised a perfect on-drive.

'Nothing.'

He practised a leg glance. 'You seen the cricket ball?'

'No,' I said. It was in a pot plant under the back stairs.

He practised a hook shot. 'I was thinking of maybe going and hitting a few balls in the nets.'

'By yourself?' I asked. He obviously wanted me to play with him. There was no way.

'Course not. Damon's gunna come later,' he said. And we might go sleuthing after that, which is another word for detecting, for your information. In the meantime you can play if you want.'

Damon!

'When did you organise this?' I asked, trying to sound like I didn't care.

'He came round this morning while you were having brekky.'

'Did he say anything about me?'

Connor looked at me as if I'd just slammed a cream pie into my own face. 'Why would he say anything about you?'

I thought he must have come because he'd wanted to give me a message.

'I'll come if I get to bat first,' I said.

'Nup. But if you bowl I'll hit catches.'

I knew he wouldn't hit catches—but it was a chance to talk to Damon.

'Fine,' I sighed, and I jumped down from the tree. 'Let's go.'

7

BROKEN GLASS

I FOLLOWED CONNOR out the front gate and past Mum's glass-bead necklace, which was still in the gutter.

'Aren't you going to pick that up?' I asked.

'I still might get clues off it. You never know, when we come back it might be gone,' said Connor.

And so we went to the nets on the oval, in the shade of the fig tree, and I soon found myself bowling and bowling and bowling without Connor hitting a single catchable catch.

I always bowled my best against Connor. But unfortunately my best was so crappy that even Connor, who was woeful against kids his own age, could smack ball after ball effortlessly into the net. 'That's a four', he'd say under his breath as he hit it, or 'excellent shot'. If I asked what he'd said he'd look innocent and say 'nothing'. And if I did manage to get him out I'd usually only last a few balls before he got me out. I don't know why I bowled and bowled at him and only stopped when I had a tantrum or he lost interest. I can only say it was because he was the big brother and I was the small one.

He'd just slogged another ball past my ankles and mumbled 'there's his fifty', and I'd just decided to hell with him and cricket in general, when I saw Damon strolling across the oval towards us.

Right, Connor, I said to myself, *you're gunna get it now, see how you like* this *one.*

I went back to my mark, and kept going till my run-up was twice as long as usual. I carefully positioned the ball between my fingers. Then, without even glancing at Damon, I tiptoed, then jogged, then charged towards Connor with all my spite. Just before my front foot hit the crease I leapt and turned side on, pointed my elbow at his head and, with the other arm, sent the ball searing down the pitch.

Connor walked up on it and executed a textbook forward defence.

The ball rolled back to me.

'Not bad. You're getting better,' he said.

Damon was laughing. He was doubled over with laughter, slapping his leg. 'What a classic,' he said.

I left the ball where it was and turned for home.

Damon said, 'Aren't you coming *sleuthing*?'

Connor said, 'His knickers are in a twist.'

'No they're not,' I said. They were, but Damon obviously wanted me to go along. So I turned back.

'I'm coming,' I said.

'Oh, great!' said Connor.

'So where do you want to go, Detective Connor?' said Damon.

'I went to the church on Sunday and there wasn't anything there. One place I haven't been is the primary school.'

Damon looked at me with a knowing grin. 'Might be worth a look. What do you reckon, Aaron?'

I'd been signalling *no* to him like crazy. 'There won't be anything there,' I said.

Connor raised an eyebrow. 'Aaron, honestly. You can come along, but just don't say anything.'

I sighed. 'Fine.'

As we made our way there Damon said, 'How's the investigation coming along?'

'Well, let's think about it logically,' said Connor. 'Someone took rosary beads from a church. What's the motive? Money.'

'Maybe people wanted them for devil worship,' said Damon.

'Could be,' said Connor.

'Or it could be church people who need them to pray with,' said Damon. "Cause they lost their own rosary beads.'

'And you know I found that religious medallion thing. And in the paper it said, 'a number of items' were stolen. I bet you a billion bucks that medallion was one of the 'items'. And you know what else the paper said? Two boys. So. We're looking for two boys.'

'Two devil-worshipper boys,' said Damon.

'That's right,' said Connor, seeing that Damon was being funny and playing along. 'Two devil-worshipper boys with no money who live near Shoe Street.'

'Why Shoe Street?' Damon asked.

'That's where I found the medallion,' Connor replied.

Damon shrugged.

By this stage we were at the primary school in the courtyard. 'We should split up—it'll make our search quicker,' said Connor. 'Aaron you check the front playground. Damon and me'll check round here.'

We split up. I spent ten minutes sitting on the

front playground monkey bars, then went back to the courtyard.

'Find anything?' asked Connor.

'Nah.'

'Hey!' said Damon, with a shocked look on his face. 'I just got this weird feeling. You didn't check the top classrooms, did you, Aaron? Well, I just got this premonition there might be something there. Should we check it out?'

'Okay,' said Connor.

When I tried to get Damon's attention to find out what the hell he was thinking, he just grinned like it was some kind of big game and he'd just made the smartest move ever.

He led the way, straight to my old classroom, and there, just as we'd left it, was the scattered broken glass of the smashed louvre.

Connor was stunned. 'Holy hell, you were right. Someone tried to break in here, too.'

'Sometimes I'm a bit psychic. Every now and then I get these really strong feelings,' said Damon.

Connor said, 'It's gotta be the thief! This is your old classroom, Aaron, right? Maybe it's someone in your class. Don't touch anything, you might stuff up the clues.' He pulled his mini plastic magnifying glass from his pocket and began to examine the jagged pieces of louvre glass.

'What are you looking for?' asked Damon, barely able to keep the laugh out of his voice.

'Bits of cloth or something from the thieves' clothes,' Connor replied.

After a while he stood up. 'Nothing. They're cleverer than I thought.'

At this Damon actually cough-laughed.

Connor didn't notice. 'So this was their first place to rob, and when they didn't find anything in here worth taking they went for the church,' he said.

'Nice theory,' said Damon.

'Maybe we should go check the church again,' said Connor.

But Damon, just like that, had lost interest. He stretched, yawned, and said, 'Nah. Let's go back to my place and watch videos.'

'Okay,' said Connor brightly, though I knew him well enough to know he was disappointed.

As we walked back, Connor seemed to be doing some heavy thinking. He kept looking at me. 'Who else lives round here who's in your class?'

'Jane Singleton?'

'I mean boys, of course.'

'Coldy?'

Connor nodded to himself. 'Coldy.'

'Oliver West?' I tried.

'He's away on holiday, remember? I don't know about you sometimes, Aaron.'

And then Stevie Harmison rode past on his bike. No helmet. He wasn't even holding the handlebars; his arms were folded in front of his chest. He was pretending he hadn't seen us. He wasn't wobbling at all, but if even a pebble had been in his path he'd have face-planted, and if a car'd come, him and his shiny smug BMX would've been as flat as toads. But of course, there were never any pebbles in Stevie Harmison's path.

'I can do that,' said Connor, which was not even almost true. He could let go of the handlebars for a microsecond, while going really slow. (We had one rickety girl's bike between us that I hardly ever rode. Technically it was Mum's.)

'I always ride like that,' said Damon. 'Still would if my bike was here.'

I said, 'What about Stevie Harmison? *He* lives on Shoe Street and he goes to the high school...*and* he's crazy.'

'Think he just went to the top of my suspects list,'

said Connor.

'I'm going home,' said Damon, 'Coming, Connor?'

'Yep,' Connor replied, and then he turned to me. 'You should go home, Aaron. I'm going over to Damon's and we're going to do big-kid stuff.'

'I'm coming,' I said.

'Well, you are not invited,' said Connor, speaking slowly like he was trying to get through to an idiot.

They started off without me.

'That's not fair,' I mumbled and I started walking home. 'I'm telling Mum,' I called over my shoulder.

'She's at work.'

I ignored him and kept walking, red faced, thinking, *Then I'll tell Peter.*

Peter had moved into our house the day before—that was the huge event.

Mum had told us over breakfast. She just came out with it. 'Guess what?'

She said he was going to stay 'for a while—it depends.' Like she'd hardly considered it. Between mouthfuls of cereal and sips of coffee. 'It'll be good to have a man around. They can fix things. I think he'll be a big help. What do you think, Connor?'

Connor shrugged. He was reading *The Lord of the Rings*.

'How about you, Aaron?'

'I mean...I think...' I'd stammered. It was impossible to say straight away; we'd only met him once, after all. It would take some serious pondering.

I was still pondering at the kitchen table forty minutes later, with a soggy half-eaten Weetbix in front of me, when Peter appeared at the back door, with his bags at his feet and an uncertain smile on his face.

'Mum,' I called.

Peter looked down the hall and called, 'Trace.'

All he'd brought was one old-fashioned suitcase and a string bag full of clothes. I sat on Mum's bed and watched him unpack.

'That bag's called a bilum. Got that in Papua New Guinea one time when we made land there,' he said.

The first thing he took out of the suitcase was a ball of newspaper. He began peeling layers off it, finally revealing a bronze-coloured metal urn.

He carefully placed it on Mum's make-up table, where it settled in comfortably among her perfume bottles.

'What's that?' I asked.

'That,' said Peter, 'is the ashes of the first boat I ever went to sea on.'

'What happened to it?'

'It sank. It burned first—there was a fire on board. Then it sank. I was on shore. I went back the next day and the only thing left was a bit of the mast washed up on the beach, so I burned it. And I had this lying round not doing anything, so I emptied it out and put the mast ashes in it.'

'But why do you carry it around with you?'

Peter thought about it for a second. 'It's to remind me that nothing in life is permanent. One day everything you've got can just be not there anymore. One day you turn around and BANG'—he clapped his hands—'there's nothing.'

Next he took out a pair of worn-out sandshoes and a pair of thongs and lined them up along the wall. Then he'd opened a drawer in Dad's chest of drawers and started putting his clothes into it.

That was yesterday. Hopefully he was home now.

I ran to the intersection and turned into our road. Peter's truck was parked on the verge outside our house. It had four sets of double wheels and a back compartment like a big removal van, and it had stickers that said 'Tennant Creek' and 'Biloela' on the back bumper, and 'Go the Cronulla Sharks', and 'No More Nukes'.

I ran on through our front gate and under our

house. Peter was at the back stairs jemmying up a rotten step, with a beer and a transistor playing grainy pop music at his feet. He was wearing a sweat-darkened blue singlet and he had a tool belt slung over his footy shorts—the tradie's uniform. But somehow he didn't look like a real tradie. Maybe it was his skinny legs, or his concentrating-too-hard face.

When he saw me he straightened up with his hands on his lower back and nodded. 'What are you up to, Aaron?' His smell was like a dead prawn left on a salty wharf.

Now, faced with it, it seemed weird to dob on Connor to someone I hardly knew.

'Nothing,' I mumbled.

Peter cleared his throat. 'Your mum's stayin' back at work for a bit so I'm gunna get tea. Come on, you.' The last bit was addressed to the step. He leaned on the crowbar and the nails groaned. The muscles in his arms strained. He cleared his throat again. 'So what do you want for tea?'

'Fish and chips.'

'Nah, we're not getting fish and chips, I'm gunna make something. Thinkin' maybe chops and potatoes and peas.'

Before I knew what was coming I blurted out,

'Connor won't let me hang out with him and Damon.'

Great. Now he'll think I'm a dobber.

Peter leaned again on the crowbar and with a loud crack the nails finally gave and the step broke free.

'Did you ask him?'

'He said no.'

Peter lifted the step away from the frame. 'Well tell him…tell him he can't play with your stuff.'

'But he *never* wants to play with my stuff.'

'Then play by yourself. Or why don't you help me here?'

Mum never asked you to help, she just told you you were helping.

I said, 'What do you want me to do?'

He pointed to the rotten step. 'You can start splittin' that up.'

He handed me a tomahawk and I got to work, hacking into the white-anted wood.

'See how soft it is? That step was gunna break any minute. It was mouldy too, like all the wood round here. Probably should replace the whole lot. Once you've got that in little bits we can make a bonfire out the back.'

I gathered up the pieces and followed Peter down the back to behind the chook pen, which was a lot less scary with someone else there. I glanced at the lemon tree—no spider. And no kid's head above the back fence.

I threw the wood onto the pile Peter had started that was squashing the high grass. And I took the opportunity to retrieve my soccer ball. Peter added some planks that had been part of an old bed he'd found under the house.

'We should pull the chook pen down, too. It's probably full of snakes. Better ask your mum first, though,' he said.

We stood, arms folded, admiring our handiwork. Peter glanced around like he was itching to dig things up, chop things down, get the place shipshape. 'About that other thing,' he said. 'You should stand up for yourself. Show him you won't let him pick on ya.'

'How do I do that? He's bigger than me.'

'Doesn't matter how big you are. When I was a kid I wasn't the biggest bloke either, but no one picked on me and that's 'cause I didn't take anyone's crap.'

As I washed my hands in the kitchen sink I considered how to not take Connor's crap. My first stupid thought was to ask Connor. If *he* wanted to get back at someone he'd think of a plan, something clever and evil. But it couldn't be *too* bad—I didn't want to put him in hospital or anything.

I got my double-sided pencil and an old exercise book and lay on my bed and thought, I could do that trick where you put a bucket of slime on a door, and when he opens the door the slime goes all over him. I drew a yellow door with a bucket of green slime on it. But would it work? And he'd know it was me straight-away. I could frame him, copy his writing and write a confession: *Hello Mum and Peter, this is Connor. I am writing to say that it was me that stole the rosary beads. I took them and buried them. I feel very guilty so I am confessing. Sorry. From Connor.*

I read it back. Obviously I couldn't use my two-coloured pencil. And it didn't sound like something Connor would write. It needed more big words. I feel *extremely* guilty?

It wouldn't work. I threw the book down.

Having not heard Connor come back, I decided I'd go look in his room for inspiration. Creeping down the back stairs was more of a challenge now that the bottom three had been replaced with the bed slats. The steps bent and shifted on their braces even under my flimsy weight.

I knocked on Connor's door.

No answer.

I went straight to his desk. The homework book was there; the 'Possibles' and 'Probables' lists was striped with red. Crossed off the 'Probables' side were: devil-worshippers', 'criminals', 'the Mafia', as were most of the 'Possibles', and there was a big question mark next to 'Priest (inside job)'. 'Stevie Harmison' had been circled and there was an exclamation mark next to it. 'Damon' was still there. 'Aaron' too. I considered crossing my name out, but saw straightaway what a dumb idea that was.

My attention was drawn to the mini Tardis on his bookshelf. Hanging off it was a key ring with a miniature Rubik's cube attached to it—he'd found it in the Woolies carpark. I put it in my pocket. Without it the room looked wrong, incomplete.

I crept back outside, carefully closing the door—I had his cube and there was absolutely nothing he could do about it.

But where to hide it? Connor would go straight to the obvious places. Then I noticed that our ladder, which was actually two separate metal ladders joined end to end, was leaning up against the house. The very first thing Peter had done after unpacking had been to scoop the leaves out of our roof gutter. Consequently, the ladder was still up and a line of dark soggy leaves surrounded the house. *The roof!* Not even Connor would think to look there.

It was only when I put my foot on the first rung that I considered how high our roof was. The ends of the ladder were so far away they seemed to join at the top. I put my foot on the second rung. It felt solid enough.

I was halfway up before a loud creak made me freeze. My pulse was thumping, and it was sixty slow seconds before I started climbing again, with my face against the rungs, holding on so tight not even a giant could have prised me off.

Going from the ladder to the roof was the hardest part—specifically the letting go of the ladder bit. I was careful not to look down. I imagined the ladder sliding sideways and I scraped my knee, but I made it.

Our roof was corrugated iron. Some sheets looked new and some were rusted, but they all creaked and they all scorched my hands and feet as I inched my way to the top. A gentle breeze with the smell of the sea in it ruffled my hair. There was St Rita's High School and St Rita's Primary School and the church not too far away, and the hospital, and past it the tops of some of the buildings of town. And behind me were the mountains of the Misty Range, hazy and unreal.

And there were the houses all around. Somehow they looked less significant from up here, like the buildings of Coldy's dad's train set, all beside the point next to the train. But there was no train in our neighbourhood. Everything down there was still, as if waiting for something, each house holding on to some secret. Holding its breath.

Then I saw it—a police car. It was on the street up from ours, next to the school, moving slowly. It stopped. Two policemen got out. Instinctively I knew they were looking for the thieves. Looking for me.

I slipped the Rubik's cube into the roof gutter. *What if it rains?* I thought as I got back on the ladder. I looked up—the sky was creamy blue with no clouds, but even so I retrieved the cube and, after climbing back down the ladder, I hid it under the top bunk mattress. Then I lay on my bed trying to imagine Connor's face when he found out I wasn't taking his crap anymore.

8

THE BLACK PANTHER

AS I LAY there on my bed I couldn't stop thinking about the police. *They're coming for you. They're probably at the front door right now—with handcuffs. Did you think you were going to get away with it, you idiot? It's all over.*

My bedroom had one door, one way in and out: once the police were in the house I was trapped. *Get out now*, yelled my brain. My self-control was slipping. *No. Wait. Calm down.* I slowed my breathing. *Just listen. If you hear them, then make your run.* I listened. The afternoon was full of noise: hammering, some mum yelling at her kids, a car door slamming. *Was that a car at our house? Was that voices, or the wind, or nothing?* I stopped breathing so I could hear better, then I breathed again. But suddenly there wasn't enough oxygen. My chest was getting squeezed, and then I was rushing out of the room, gasping, through the kitchen, down the back stairs. My eyes went to the avocado tree, and then the Datsun, but they were just places to wait before I got caught. I needed to get *away*. *Far away*: Polly's Creek, the bush, the hollow with the sheet of corrugated iron over it.

I slipped over the wire fence in front of the chook pen into Mrs Melchiori's place. Her yard was totally shaded by mango trees so hardly any grass grew there. I commando rolled and darted my way from tree to tree and under her back awning. Then I hurdled her other side fence and found myself on Shoe Street. I couldn't see the police, but I felt as exposed as hell with nothing to hide behind.

I started to run.

Immediately I realised that was a bad idea—I was drawing more attention to myself—but I couldn't stop.

By the time I *had* to stop, my hands on my knees, nearly about to vomit, I was at the T-intersection in front of Damon's house. It was a little house on stilts with a corrugated-iron roof and walls. A deflated basketball was stuck in its roof gutter and had been for years, since long before Damon had moved there.

I ran up the stairs and knocked on the door.

No answer. Maybe he was still off somewhere with Connor.

Come on, Damon, answer the door.

I tried one last knock, then ran down the stairs, and kept running, past the vacant lot that led to the swamp, past the yard that was full of chooks, past the big yellow house that doubled as a daycare centre, past Anne Mitchell's house. Anne Mitchell was in Connor's class. Her Chihuahua—whose name was Coco, don't ask me how I knew that—barked at me.

After a while I came to where the houses ended. Across the road was sugar cane, and beyond it I could see the blue-green of rainforest-covered hills: the foothills of the Misty Range. Polly's Creek was at the base of those hills. If I ran across maybe three or four cane fields, I'd be on Polly's Creek Road.

Okay. Wow. I'm really going to do this. Going to leave the world behind, live in a hole under a bit of tin, eat fish and never talk to anyone ever again.

An old lady was digging in her front garden, and a man was hammering something on his roof. I scanned the road one last time for police, then scampered across and ducked between the rows of tall sugar cane.

In among the cane it was close and hot. I had to

brush the sharp-edged leaves away from my face as I went along. Though the path was straight I couldn't see more than a metre ahead. I bent down and sort of crouch-jogged.

I was near the middle of the first field when I realised I was being followed.

I stopped.

All I could hear was the flitter of the tops of the cane in the breeze. But I knew something was there. Watching me.

I said, 'Who's there?'

The cane sighed in answer.

On a hunch, I said, 'Is that...the panther?'

The feeling of being watched intensified, even though I'd made the black panther up. Letting my imagination go too far, as usual. There was, of course, no panther. And therefore nothing following me. I took a few steps. It, whatever it was, took a few steps. I turned around. I heard a rustle, the sound of whatever it was turning its large body in the thin path between the cane next to mine, and I began to run back the way I had come, with the cane scratching my arms and face.

Then I was out of the field again, with the road in front of me, the houses, the old lady gardening, the man hammering, dogs barking, like there was nothing out of the ordinary anywhere in the world.

I crossed the road again, my heart still scurrying, and made for home.

I'd have made a terrible fugitive anyway: I'd never started a fire by myself, never gutted a fish. I was addicted to TV. I would've been lucky to last an hour in the bush.

The business about the panther was just me freaking out; after all, black panthers were from Africa or somewhere. North Queensland was totally the wrong habitat. An actual black panther in Fingleton would've sweated to death in a day. And the police probably weren't even looking for me. It was time to get serious; time to be like Connor and think logically.

I took a deep breath, and then let it out. Deep breathing was good too. After a few more deep breaths, and all that logic, I was already beginning to feel a lot better.

That afternoon Mum came home after all and we were in the kitchen discussing dinner. Peter was still intending to cook.

'You ever turned a stove on before?' Mum asked.

Connor had his face in *The Lord of the Rings*. He hadn't said a word all afternoon.

'How hard can it be?' said Peter who was leaning back on his chair, as if he was a part of the place already. It must be nicer for him living here than on a prawn trawler, I thought. much better than getting wet the whole time, and any minute you might hit a whale and sink.

We were having potatoes, carrots and steak—medium rare. The decision was made.

'By the way, what happened to the back stairs?' said Mum.

Peter cleared his throat. 'They were rotten. There's a few more that need to go. I'll finish it off tomorrow morning.'

'Why didn't you get new stairs first? Someone's gunna go straight through one of those things and break their neck,' said Mum.

'I'm getting new ones tomorrow morning,' said Peter.

'Ya nong,' said Mum, teasing.

'Nong, am I?' Peter jumped up and flicked her bum with the wooden spoon. Mum turned on him and a play fight erupted: him all elbows, fending her off, grabbing at her hips; her squealing, one hand guarding her hair; both of them putting on a show for Connor and me.

Connor kept his face in his book.

Then Mum told me to get her handbag out of the car and the play fight was over. Peter sniffed, rubbed his nose, and wandered out to the back stairs for a smoke.

After his cigarette he started cooking. Peter cooked with a series of jerky movements and whispered swear words. The vegetable water hissed as it boiled over. He snatched it off the stove and it splashed on the floor, and he snapped 'Yes!' when Mum said, 'You right, Peter?'

Finally he put the plates proudly onto the table, and Connor put his book down. I studied him for signs he'd missed his Rubik's cube, but he was stony-faced, off in some other world as usual.

Peter chewed loudly, talked with his mouth full, licked his knife. When the conversation turned to cars he frowned and said, 'A ute is the way to go. 'Cause we're going to want to take stuff to the tip every now and then. Hilux maybe.' And he started throwing around terms like *cylinders*, and *diesel*, leaving me and Connor and Mum far behind.

'Me old man taught me about cars. I could change a tyre before I could walk,' he said. 'I'll have to get these two up to speed. Whatdya reckon?'

Mum said, 'What do you think, boys?'

I said, 'I reckon.'

Connor, reading again, said nothing.

After dinner Connor and I were on the floor in front of the TV and Peter was on the couch and *Magnum P.I.* was about to start. And then Mum, in her nightie, came in saying, 'I can't take it anymore,' and snapped the TV off. 'It's a beautiful night. We're going outside.'

'I'm not,' said Connor.

'*I* know,' said Mum. 'Let's take the fruit salad.'

'In the dark?' said Peter.

'There aren't any monsters, Peter. Connor get the big blanket out of the spare room. Should we get a torch for Peter? Here, make yourself useful,' she said, and she passed Peter the bowl of fruit salad.

Peter rolled his eyes.

Connor said, 'She's always like this.'

And then we trooped down the back stairs into the backyard and onto a blanket spread on the damp grass. There was a yellow glow from the kitchen window, and the sounds of Mrs Melchiori's TV, and night insects as tiny as grains of sand hovering around us and landing in the fruit salad.

We watched for shooting stars but they had seen us

coming and were lying low.

'Isn't this better than being cooped up inside? We used to do this all the time when I was a kid,' said Mum.

Connor said, 'Anybody else getting bitten?'

'Okay, everyone has to tell a story,' said Mum. 'Have you got one, Aaron?'

'No,' I said, which was true. I couldn't think of one, but also, I wasn't speaking to Connor because he'd gone off with Damon and left me out, and telling a story seemed a lot like speaking to him.

'Don't look at *me*,' said Peter. He'd brought some cushions from the couch and had propped himself up on them, with his fingers intertwined on his belly and his beer settled in the grass beside him.

'Come on, Peter, you've got tons of stories. Why don't you tell a fishing one?'

But then Connor said, 'I've got one,' and he launched into a story about a boy who lived in a kingdom with elves and magic swords and a wizard and lots of creatures jumping out from behind things.

Mum wriggled closer to Peter.

And then abruptly Connor said, 'And that's the end of the story.'

Mum sat up. 'Great story, Connor. Now, how about a fishing story?'

Peter said, 'It's getting late, ay?'

'All right, go in if you want,' Mum said.

No sooner had she said it than Peter was juggling his cushions and beer up the back stairs with Connor behind him, Mum not far behind Connor, and me not far behind Mum. I didn't want to be left alone in the dark yard, but actually I didn't want to go inside because a story had finally popped into my head.

At first I'd thought of telling the story of the night Mum had crashed our Datsun, but I thought Mum probably wouldn't want to hear that story. Then I remembered one Gran had told about Dad one time when we were over her place.

I'd been sitting on the carpet in front of Gran's TV. On her side table she had a framed photo of a thin, hairy-legged man with a moustache leaning against a brick wall with his arms folded and looking into the lens with an *I'm not saying cheese for no one* expression on his face. My dad.

In an ad break Gran had put her knitting down and said, 'Did I ever tell you boys about your dad's little adventure at the Greek festival down at Mission Beach?'

It was the Festival of the Ascension—we used to go. I remembered lining up for a sausage in a slice of white bread, and a plastic cup of green cordial. I remembered kids playing tiggy and me pretending I didn't want to. I remembered Connor with his book and Mum with her wine and her big straw hat.

'Every year the priest throws a gold cross into the water,' Gran began. 'And the young men swim out to try to get it, and whoever finds the cross gets good luck for a year. For some reason only Greek boys are allowed to do it.

'Well, one year when your father was about twenty, just like in the photo, he and Stewey Lum and Greg Bracewell were there, all havin' a good laugh, and they went down on the beach with everyone to watch the ceremony. They stood quietly.' Here she smiled through her glasses as she remembered. 'But when the priest threw the cross and all those Greek boys jumped in, well your father couldn't resist—he just loved a race. He let out a yell and chased after them, and he overtook them all and got the cross. He was the first non-Greek ever to do it.

'They didn't like it,' she said, 'the Greeks, but what could they do? They tried to ban him from going again, but if you could have been there, if you could have seen how strong he was then, the way he swam...' She shook her head and she sighed.

'Did he get luck out of it?' I asked.

'Well, that was the year that Connor was born,' she said and she patted Connor on the head.

Mum had been quiet on the way home after the story. Probably she was doing what I was doing, which was thinking about Dad.

9
A PLAN

IT WAS WEDNESDAY. A *Fingleton Gazette* day.

Peter said, 'Might have a trucker's breakfast.'

After a bit Mum said, 'What's that?'

'Dry two-minute noodles and tomato sauce,' Peter replied.

I said, 'Gross.'

'You can't be fussy if your truck's out in the middle of nowhere,' said Peter, pleased. 'Anyway, don't knock it till you've tried it.'

'You don't get it, Mum. I don't *want* the paper, I'm saying I actually *need* it,' said Connor. 'It could change my entire investigation.'

'Connor, I am working this morning and I'd like some peace. So you'll just have to wait.' Mum sipped her coffee. Then she said, 'Or if you ask nicely, maybe

Peter might take you.'

'Really?' Connor turned to Peter, who shrugged.

'I was going into town anyway. If we take the Mini you guys can tag along,' he said and then turned to Mum. 'That okay, Trace?'

'Sure.'

'Great. Let's go then,' said Connor.

'Wait on,' said Peter. He rinsed his bowl at the sink, disappeared, and then reappeared with a new-looking football, which he threw from hand to hand. 'First things first. Come on, you boys, let's go pass the footy round.'

Connor said, 'Do we have to?'

'If you want to go into town you do,' said Mum. 'Now go on. It'll be good for you.'

'Just gunna impart some of me wisdom on 'em, Trace,' said Peter, sounding like he'd rehearsed it in his head.

Mum said, 'So you won't be long, then?'

No one answered her.

On the walk over the road Peter said, 'Who do you blokes support?'

Connor shrugged. Connor and I didn't know anything about football—not even the rules. I couldn't think of a single team.

'I'm a Sharks supporter. They're playing tonight,' said Peter. 'We'll have to watch the game. If youse want you can be Sharks supporters too. Or it might be more fun if we've got different teams. So Aaron, you could be the Roosters, and Connor, you could be Parramatta. If you want. Or maybe we'll watch a few games first and then you can decide.'

'What colour is Parramatta?' I asked.

'Blue and yellow.'

'They're my favourite colours.'

Connor rolled his eyes. 'Yeah, that's the most crucial thing, Aaron,' he said.

When we got to the oval we formed a triangle and passed the footy to each other for a while. Then Peter said, 'Okay, now go right out and I'll kick it to you and you kick it back.'

He took the ball in both hands, looked up at us, looked down at the ball, back up again, then threw it up and sort of stabbed his foot at it, and the ball wobbled through the air, and I had to run twenty metres to get it.

After Peter ran to get one of my kicks he put his hands on his knees and started coughing, and then every time he ran he coughed, and once he spat something out and I found it: a grey goo ball that glooped disgustingly to the grass like a stranded jellyfish.

We'd only been at it ten minutes when Peter said between gasps, 'Youse had enough? Call it a day?'

We went home and all had showers.

Later, as we drove Gran's Mini to town, out of nowhere Peter said, 'You know you don't have to call me Peter. Makes me sound like a pommy. Pete's what me mates call me.'

'Okay, Pete,' I said.

'Can we stop and get the paper first?' said Connor.

'Nah, mate, I wanna get those steps sorted out first. Won't be long.'

We stopped at the hardware shop, and while Pete was talking to the hardware bloke, who was a mate of his, I wandered through the sawdusty aisles of paint tins wondering why there were a hundred shades of white and brown but no purple or orange, but also thinking about the rosary beads.

Logically, as far as I could see, I had three options. Option one—turn myself in to the police. Consequences? Mum would kill me. People would throw rotten tomatoes at me as I walked down the street and old ladies would spit on me. And Damon would be busted too, because once I'd started confessing I knew I'd blab everything.

Option two was a bit weak—confess to the priest in the little room at the back of the church with the opening like a letterbox: *Bless me, Father, for I have sinned. I broke into your room and took your rosary beads.* Priests weren't allowed to tell secrets, but did that include when a crime had been committed?

Option three...let's see. Hmm...

If Damon did sell the rosary beads on the black market like he'd said he would, I could give my half of the money to Mum and tell her I'd found it and then she could buy a car with it.

Pete and the bloke were still talking low, serious man talk. Now they were examining a plank of wood from a shelf in the back warehouse. I walked out the front.

Connor was in the front seat of the Mini reading *The Lord of the Rings*.

'They haven't got any purple paint,' I said through the window.

'Who'd want to paint their house purple?' Connor replied without looking up, and I saw at once that he was right.

I've got your Rubik's cube, smart-arse, I thought to myself. But I'd taken the Rubik's cube a day ago and he still hadn't noticed. Taking it had been a mistake;

I should have taken something he'd miss, like one of his books. Like *The Lord of the Rings*, his favourite.

Pete came out. 'They're gunna cut us some steps tomorrow. Looks like we'll have to put up with the old bed planks for a bit longer.'

'Can we get the paper now?' said Connor.

'Bottle shop first. It's just round the corner,' Pete replied.

Connor sighed.

At the bottle shop Pete picked up six cartons of beer. The bottle shop guy helped load them into our boot and onto the back passenger seat.

After the bottle shop we went to the newsagent and finally bought the paper. Then we went to Woolies and bought some beans, steak and potatoes for tea, and some fishing line from a bargain bin.

At home we unloaded the beer.

'You blokes take the groceries upstairs, ay?' said Pete as he began to walk out the gate.

'Where are you going?'

'I'm just gunna duck back into town to sort some stuff out. Tell your Mum I won't be two ticks, ay?'

'Okay.'

Connor grabbed the paper and kept it tight in his armpit as we took the groceries inside and as he made himself a cup of coffee and sat at the kitchen table. He disarmpitted the paper then and shook it like they do in the movies. Then he opened it, turned a few pages and read for a bit. His eyes widened, and under his breath he said, 'Cool.'

I said, 'Show us.'

'Not yet.'

'I want to do the crossword.'

He looked at me with his eyebrows raised.

I pressed on. 'My teacher said we should do it on the holidays for our vocabulary.'

He shook his head. 'You're weird,' he said, but he threw me the paper.

After that I felt like I had to actually do the cross-word while I ate a slice of bread.

'Nine down—a phrase containing words of opposite or different meanings.'

'Oxymoron,' said Connor, who couldn't help himself.

'How do you spell it?'

'O. X. Y. You should be able to spell moron, seeing as though you are one.'

I turned to the Police Round-up: *A bicycle was stolen from the bicycle rack in front of the Ernest Street bus station. The bicycle was a red BMX-style with coloured beads on its spokes. Anyone with any information please call Crime Stoppers.*

Andrea Clegg had a bike like that. She probably hadn't even chained it up.

Mum came up the back stairs with a shirtfront full of oranges. She emptied them on the sideboard and said, 'Where's Peter?'

'Went back into town.'

She got the electric juicer out of the cupboard. 'Into town? Did he say how long he'd be?'

'Two ticks,' said Connor.

'A person who rules China.'

'Emperor.'

I pretended to write 'Emperor' but kept reading the Police Round-up: *A thirty-six-year-old man was charged with assault following an altercation outside the Grand Hotel with a hotel security individual, who sustained injuries to his hands. The charged man was remanded in custody.*

Gggrrrrrrrrriindd went the first half-orange. 'But he said he's coming back for dinner, right?' Mum went on.

And then I came to the last entry: 'Church Broken Into'.

A wave of nausea hit me. There was no way I was

going to be able to read it in front of Mum and Connor. 'Might go finish the crossword in my room,' I said.

Gggrrrrrrrrriindd. 'You had lunch?' Mum asked.

'Yep,' I replied and I ran to my room, to my bed, and read the last entry. And read it again. Two brief sentences:

Church Broken Into

Following the recent theft at the St Rita's Catholic Church police will be door-knocking nearby households. Anyone with information please call Crime Stoppers.

So that was that. I was screwed.

Oxymoron. I found I'd been doodling the word on the edge of the newspaper. Then I wrote, *Thief.* I tried it with the *i* and *e* switched. It looked wrong. I wrote it backwards. Then I wrote *I am a thief* backwards. Then *I stole the rosary beads* backwards. Then forwards. Over and over. Then I tore off that bit of paper and put it in my mouth and chewed it, gluey and inky, then swallowed it. I needed someone to talk to, but there was no one. Obviously I couldn't ask Connor. Mum? *You did what? We're going to the police station. Now!* she'd say.

The boy behind the back fence? But I didn't even

know his name, or how long he'd lived there, or if his dad was a cop. And there was the way he said fuck—he was a 'cool kid'. I said fuck quietly to myself a few times. That would have to do.

I went out into the backyard and kicked the soccer ball around, keeping one eye on the back fence. After a few minutes I called out, 'Oi!'

No answer.

There were some green baby oranges under the orange trees, I picked one up and threw it at the fence. It gave a satisfying *tock*. I threw another one. I called out 'Oi' again. When there was still no answer I went back to my room and read the Police Round-up one more time.

The TV guide said the Sharks were playing the Panthers at 7:30. Me, Mum and Connor never watched footy, though most boys in my class did. But when 7:30 came and Connor and I were plonked in front of the TV, Pete was still nowhere to be seen. The whistle blew and someone kicked the ball and the person who caught it got tackled and then someone else got tackled. I tried to follow along, but it wasn't clear to me why anyone was doing anything. After a while Connor wandered back to the kitchen and I followed him.

Still no Pete. We sat by the clock radio that sat on

the sideboard between the phone and our fat-tummied statue of Buddha.

'8:35,' said Connor.

'8:36,' I said.

'8:37,' said both of us simultaneously.

'That'll do,' said Mum with enough irritation in her voice to make us stop. She ended up making toasted cheese-and-tomato sandwiches, which Connor and I ate in front of *The Love Boat* while she and her cup of tea sat in the kitchen.

I was in bed when I heard two clumsy sets of footsteps on the back stairs, followed by the creak of the back door being guiltily opened. The TV snapped off, and then I heard Mum's quick footsteps. Then silence.

Then Mum's voice, high-pitched, and Pete's, kind of muffled. And a third voice, a man. Footsteps heavy down the stairs, Mum's voice getting louder, Pete's voice raised.

I thought, *Don't get too angry, Mum. Don't make him go yet, he only just got here.*

Then there was a crash. A plate?

'How dare you bring that drunk into my house,' I heard her shout.

Silence.

'You want to go too? Because if you want you can piss off.'

Silence.

'You *knew* I had kids. Don't you laugh at me.'

I wished Connor was still in the top bunk. I wondered if he could hear anything from his room downstairs. There was more yelling, more crashing. I pulled my pillow over my ears.

I woke up to the sound of morning birds and radio blather, and when I crept out I was surprised to find the kitchen cleaner than usual and smelling of detergent. The dishes that had been drying next to the sink had been put away, but the biggest change was in the fridge—it was nearly empty. Missing were: the jar of mango chutney, the leftover spaghetti, the wine bottle we kept our water in. The tomato sauce. And there was no beer—there'd been at least two six-packs when I'd gone to bed.

Connor came up the back stairs and sat at the table without saying anything.

'Good morning,' sang Mum, breezing in like she'd been up since six. 'Sleep well, you two?' She kissed me on the forehead.

Pete came in. 'Morning everyone,' he said, smiling

ruefully at me.

'Morning, Pete,' I said.

'Morning, Peter,' said Mum.

He bent down and they kissed, briefly, on the lips. It was the first time I'd seen them kiss.

We ate breakfast accompanied by the radio, the clink of cutlery on the plates, cleared throats, cereal crunched, loud swallows and the smile frozen on Mum's face.

The phone rang, and when I answered a gruff voice said, 'Pete there, mate?'

Pete took the phone with a frown. 'Pete here,' he said in a voice quicker and deeper than usual. 'Yep.' Pause. 'Yep.' Pause. 'Yep, nup, no worries. Be there in ten.'

He hung up, jumped up from his chair, ignoring Mum's 'What's up, Pete?' and disappeared down the hall. Then he was back, with his bilum slung over his shoulder.

'Got a job,' he said as he swigged his coffee. He folded his bacon and eggs into a toast sandwich, which leaked yolk onto his beard as he stuffed it in his mouth.

'How long's it gunna take?' asked Mum, but Pete's answer was too egg-muffled for me to understand. He poured himself another coffee and tried to kiss Mum with his cheeks bulging, but she arched away in his grasp and gave a little squeal of horror, which he answered with a monster's growl.

We followed Pete down to the truck.

He took a final swig of his coffee, then left the cup on the gatepost and jumped up into the cab. 'You boys be good for your Mum,' he said.

Mum stretched up to him and they whispered. Then he started the engine, and in a spit of gravel he was gone and we were left standing in front of the house.

'There he goes,' said Mum to no one. 'He'll be back soon,' she added.

I said, 'How soon?'

'Six days.'

'Wish it was longer,' said Connor, 'I think I hate him more than I've ever hated anyone in my whole life.' He said it in a matter-of-fact way, and he was surprised when Mum wrenched him by his arm.

'How dare you!' she yelled, without looking to see who was in the street to hear her.

'What?'

'Apologise, now.'

'I'm sorry,' he said. His tone was, *There, are you happy?*

'You think it's funny? There's *nothing* wrong with Peter.' She pulled on Connor's arm again, but she'd regained control, and after telling him in a low voice to, 'Get inside, *now*!' she led him back to the house. Probably she was going to make him a Milo and sit with him as he drank it—I could just picture them—and patiently explain to him that what he'd said was wrong. And he'd nod, and not actually *say* sorry, but she'd hug him anyway and that would be it. And neither of them would mention it again.

With nothing better to do I wandered into the backyard and threw some more green oranges at the back fence.

'Hey.' The boy's head appeared behind the chook pen.

I said, 'Hey, yourself.'

He had brownish skin, curly hair, and his eyes were squinting because the sun was in them. When he scratched his nose he had to let go of the top of the fence and he nearly fell out of sight.

'What's your name?' I asked.

'Byron.'

'I'm Aaron. Do you live behind there?'

'Yep. Since I was born.'

'Me too. It's weird I never knew you lived there. What school do you go to?'

'Central. How about you?'

'St Rita's. Do you know Stevie Harmison? Coldy?'

At each name he shook his head.

'And you didn't know I lived here?' I said.

He shrugged. 'Why would I?'

'Is your dad a cop?'

'Nah. He works for the council. What's your dad do?'

'He's a stuntman,' I said.

'You got brothers and sisters?'

'I got a big brother. He's a wanker.'

'I got two brothers. They're all right,' said Byron.

That made me ashamed—you defend your own flesh and blood. *Blood's thicker than water*, Mum had said once. *You two look out for each other.*

But I'd found out what I needed to—his dad wasn't a cop.

'Hey, I was wondering something.' I moved closer. 'A *friend* of mine'—*Good thinking, Aaron*, I thought—'took something. A toy. From a toy shop. Now he doesn't know what to do. He thinks maybe he should tell the police.'

Byron said, 'He should just take it back to the shop.'

Take it back to the shop. There it was—option three.

'That's not a bad idea,' I said.

Go to the swamp, get the rosary beads and the wine,

take them back to the church. So simple. What was I waiting for?

I said, 'I'm gunna go tell him,' and then I was running, through the yard, out the front gate, filled with sudden purpose. I had a plan, an actual, sensible plan!

I ran along Shoe Street till I was too puffed and had to stop. I jogged for a while, then ran again.

Soon I was passing Damon's house, through the vacant lot, through the high grass of the swamp to the clearing.

I had the beads in my hand before it occurred to me that I'd have to go back through the church all by myself. In the middle of the day. And more importantly, Damon would know what I'd done. Obviously. He'd know what a chicken I was. But there wasn't any other way. I'd just have to deal with it—

'Oi!' yelled Damon.

I ducked.

He was in his backyard. I could see his head through the grass. He was looking my way, and I ducked again, and as I did he yelled, 'Oi,' again and I heard him running. I chucked the beads back up the drain and scrambled up the bank and threw myself into the long grass with my hands over my head. And I stayed scrunched up in a ball, waiting, trying not to breathe, and thinking, *I must be so obvious.* But it was too late to hide anywhere else.

I heard the grass along the track rustling. I heard him slide down the bank.

'Is anyone there?' he said.

One minute passed, two minutes. Was he still in the clearing? It was so quiet my heart pumping was the loudest sound.

More rustling in the grass on the track.

I waited. My joints were aching from being in one position for so long. *Surely he's gone by now. Surely he's not there waiting for me.*

I crawled carefully forward, and put my face out into the track. There was no one there.

Head down, I scampered through the vacant lot.

Out on Shoe Street I ran as fast as I could, expecting a yell from behind but none came.

I ran upstairs and turned on the TV. *Had he seen me?* He would have called my name if he'd seen me, right? If he hadn't, I'd been incredibly lucky. He'd be watching the drain now for sure, I couldn't go back right away; I'd have to try again tomorrow. And I'd have to be more careful. *I'll get up as early as I can. I'll crawl along the track on my belly, or maybe I'll crawl the whole way through the vacant lot on my belly.*

Tomorrow morning, first thing.

I just had one more day to get through until it was all over. I could survive one more day.

10

BAIT FOR THE BARRA

I WENT TO bed early, but Mum had the TV too loud—some cop movie with tyres screeching and lots of gunfire—and I got thinking, and then I couldn't stop thinking. I couldn't sleep for ages.

A nightmare that I was drowning brought me suddenly awake. My sheet was a crumpled knot at the end of my bed. The fan whirred as it swept from my head to my feet, paused as a cog fell into place with a click, then swept back. Insects chirruped from the mandarin trees. A car approached. The headlights glowed for a moment on my window, then they were gone, and everything was darker than before.

When I woke up the sun was already high in the sky. *No excuses*, I thought, *This is it. Get the rosary beads, take them to church, get back before anyone knows you're gone, then toast and honey and orange juice for breakfast.*

But a surprise was waiting for me in the kitchen. Pete was sitting at the table, his neck and right arm sunburnt and smelling of Mum's pawpaw ointment.

'How goes it, mate? Second half of the job got cancelled. Got in about four,' he said and he leaned back in his chair, balancing a mug on his chest. 'Next job's not for a few days, they reckon. So, Aaron, what do you reckon about doin' some fishing?'

I felt my heart sink. 'Sure, but…when?' I said.

'Just have to wait for Connor to get up.'

Right on cue Connor appeared, his hair just-woke-up crazy. He stopped and blinked when he saw Pete.

'Want to come fishing, Connor? We're goin' soon,' said Pete.

'What about Mum?'

'She said it's all right. She's sleeping in.'

He shrugged. 'Okay.'

'Could I quickly go and do something first?' I asked.

'What do you want to do?' said Pete.

I didn't know what to say, so I said, 'Nah, it's all right,' like it was no big deal. 'It can wait.'

So Connor and I had breakfast while Pete

rummaged around downstairs. When we finished he was waiting for us with two buckets and a shovel at the banana trees along the back fence.

'Now this here's the best bait in the world,' he said. He plunged the shovel into the trunk of a fallen banana tree, then kneeled down and pulled a long thin worm from the slime between the fleshy onion-like layers.

'There you go. Put some dirt in that bucket for 'em, Aaron,' he said. 'Then get down here and help me. We'll need a few.'

The worms liked the rottenest layers where the blackest slime was. Soon we had thirty banana worms, five earthworms and one witchetty grub, and black slime was caked in dark moons under my fingernails.

We got thongs and hats, and then we piled into Gran's car, Connor in the front.

'Are we going to the secret spot?' I said.

'Nup, that's a whole-day job. Gotta prepare your mum for that. Today we're just gettin' the bait. Can't catch barra with worms. The worms are to get the mudcod.'

'So they're bait for the bait,' said Connor.

'Yep.'

'Bait for the bait for the barra,' I added.

'Bait for the bait for the barra for the barby. For

your belly,' said Pete with a snort.

'For the bog.'

'For your bum,' I said. That was the last B anyone thought of.

Pete revved along our street in second till the gears screamed, then rammed it up to third, got to sixty only to hit the brakes at the corner and then speed up again. Connor caught my eye in the rear-view mirror. Pete noticed, and he didn't slow down round the next corner. The tyres squealed, we slid on our seats. I yelled out, 'Hold on.'

Connor said, 'You drive like a race-car driver.'

Pete smiled at that.

We were on the highway, with cane fields and farmhouses flashing by. A grey-haired farmer in his ute in front of us slowed us up.

'Pass him, Pete,' I yelled, and Connor started commentating, '...and number five is second now, only one car in front. The finish line is just around the corner.'

Pete put his foot down and we zoomed past the ute, cheering.

'But,' said Connor pointing to a distant car, 'there's one *more* car in front of number five after all.'

'Have to settle for second,' said Pete as we turned down a side road, which, after a kilometre or so, changed from bitumen to gravel.

We stopped before a wooden bridge over a green river shaded by clumps of bamboo that grew on both banks. Connor and I leaned against the car while Pete got a machete from the boot and cut three stalks of bamboo and trimmed the leaves and tips.

'Bamboo makes good rods. See how they bend?' He bent one rod down on itself.

'*Bamboo* to get the bait to get the barra,' I said.

We tied pieces of fishing line onto each rod and onto these Pete tied miniature hooks he got out of a rusted tin box. Then we loaded the rods into the Mini, with the ends poking out of the front passenger window, and continued heading away from the highway.

We pulled over a little way further along. It was quiet; just the engine tapping as it cooled, and the rustling of the sugar cane that stretched away from us on both sides of the road.

Connor and I took a rod each while Pete, with his rod underarm, took the worm and fish buckets and led us along a tractor-way between two cane fields. A breeze swept the tops of the cane above us but didn't even ruffle our hair let alone cool us down. My thongs were slippery. Prickles scratched my ankles. The sky was blue and clear.

'Not long now, fellas,' said Pete.

The sugar cane ended abruptly at a wall of rainforest that radiated coolness.

Pete said, 'Creek's in there. Flows into a drain, goes under the cane and comes out at Nind's Creek. Good fishing spot there, so should be something up in here.'

Connor and I took our hats off and sat in the shade of the rainforest while Pete walked up and back looking for the entrance to the track.

'Here we go,' he said before dodging through a skirt of vines and disappearing, then calling us after him.

When we stepped through the vines, it was like a switch had been flicked—the morning light turned to gloom, and the canefield sounds were replaced by the croaking of toads and the whirring of cicadas and the occasional low whistle of a bird. The track was wet with rotting leaves. We followed it single file, ducking branches and brushing away vines. We climbed over a log covered with moss and yellow mushrooms, then stepped through a patch of knee-high ferns, trying not to imagine that each whisper in the undergrowth was a snake hiss.

After about ten minutes we came to a place where a fallen tree had torn down a mess of vines and light poured through the hole in the canopy above. Here we caught our breath, wiped sweat from our faces, watched a butterfly crisscross the sunlight, and listened to the *dooooo-wop* call of some bird I didn't know the name of. No one said anything: it was a place where talking about things like if your foot was sore or what show had been on TV the night before would have felt wrong. I thought, *One hundred years ago there would have been rainforest like this everywhere, even where our house is. And it'd been there forever. And then we came along.* And then I thought, *If I have to hide, this is where I'll come. This is much better than Polly's Creek.*

The fallen tree was too big to climb over so we edged round it, but we couldn't find the track on the other side. We kept pushing on, further into the forest.

Suddenly a pond appeared before us. It was the size of a backyard pool. Most of it was covered by lily pads the size of dinner plates, some clean-edged, some rough-edged like something had been nibbling on them. A huge strangler fig grew on the far bank. Its branches spread above the pond sending roots straight down to dip like fingers into the water, before continuing on over our heads to blend in with the canopy. Vines twisted from branch to branch, here and there hooping down like swings.

'Who would've thought this place was in here,' said Connor, and though he didn't say it loudly it cut the still air.

Pete whispered, 'Quiet, mate, they can hear us, you know.' He took my rod, unwrapped the line, got a worm from the bucket, pulled it in half and hooked it on. Then he drew me closer. 'Go round there, mate,' he said pointing. 'Find a spot where there's not too many lily pads. She'll float down a bit, then Bob's your uncle. Be ready, hold it with both hands, could be some big ones in there.'

I followed the bank, squeezing between tree trunks. Most gaps between the lily pads were choked with green, cottonwool-like weed, but I found a spot and cast my worm. It slapped onto a lily pad, and when I lifted my rod it slid along, slipped into the water and drifted down into the blackness, and disappeared.

I waited. Connor and Pete had their lines in and they were side by side, both intently watching the water. There was a swampy, rotting smell but also a honey smell from flowers in the canopy. Everything seemed quieter around the pond. There were no bird-calls; even the cicadas sounded distant.

Pete's rod bent double. It shook as he pulled back. 'This is how it's done,' he said. With a splash a glint of silver-brown broke struggling from the water.

'Great one, Pete,' shouted Connor. 'Excellent!'

Pete dropped his rod, grabbed the fish with both hands and threw it in the bucket which he'd already half-filled with water from the pond.

I scrambled over to take a look. It was brown, had a wide, flat head with bug eyes. Its fins softly undulated, holding its teardrop-shaped body steady at the bottom of the bucket.

'What is it, Pete?' I asked.

'A mudcod. Slimy mongrels. You had any bites, Aaron?'

I shook my head.

'Give it a jiggle, that gets 'em going sometimes. How about you, Connor?'

'Nothing at all,' said Connor.

'They're in there,' said Pete. 'Let's see if we can get three each.' He re-baited, and it got quiet again, but it was a different kind of quiet now we knew we could really catch something. I held my rod tight, hardly breathing. We were all rock-still, like statues left behind at an overgrown temple. As I stared into the wedge of water where my bait had disappeared I began to notice vague shapes: clouds of weed and, further down on a bed of leaves, so faint at first I thought I was imagining it, a pinhead of pink. It was my bait. It was near a long shape too straight to be just a stick. Was it a bit of pipe? Too thin. An old fishing rod someone had dropped? A spear?

There was a fish, a big one, moving slowly towards my bait. And there were more behind it, tons of them, crowding the water. I held my breath as my bait disappeared, then let it out as the bait reappeared, untouched, and the fish were gone.

'I just saw a big school of mudcod,' I called out.

'They don't go in schools,' said Pete.

'But I saw them!'

Connor gasped. There was a splash, and then a mudcod was flapping on the end of his line just like Pete's.

'Beauty, Connor. In the bucket with it,' said Pete.

I couldn't see my bait again. Thinking it had sunk into the leaves, I tugged on the line.

The line tugged back.

'Pete! I've got one,' I yelled.

'Well, pull him up then,' said Pete.

I pulled. It held. I prayed, *Just let him come up, don't let him off. Just don't let him get under a snag.*

And then it was out of the water and wriggling on the bank beside me. It was almost as long as my forearm, easily the biggest fish I'd ever caught.

'It's a huge one, Pete.'

'Bring 'im here.'

I grabbed it in two hands and carried it over to Pete who unhooked it and dropped it in the bucket.

I looked down at our three fish. Mine was the smallest one.

'They're huge,' I said. These were just the bait. How big were the barra going to be?

'We need a few more yet, mate,' said Pete.

This time I baited my own hook.

'Got one,' yelled Connor.

I caught my second fish, unhooked it myself and threw it into the bucket. Then I got another worm, but by that time Connor had yelled, 'Got another one, Pete.'

'You're a natural, Connor,' said Pete, which got my back up because I was only one fish behind. I thought, *I'll show you who's a natural.* That was when I, we, went a little crazy. Like a feeding frenzy. And the fish bit so quick—you got a fish, slipped it off the hook, threw it in the bucket, got another worm into the water and *Bam!* Another fish.

'Getting close to enough now, I reckon, fellas.'

'Aw, Pete. Can't we get a few more?' said Connor.

'Please, Pete?' I added.

Pete looked down into the bucket. He must have seen a lot of fish in there. He rubbed his beard. 'Maybe just one or two more.'

'Yay!' said Connor.

We baited up again. Lines in. Other types of fish appeared: sleek ones with rainbow stripes. They nibbled my bait but they weren't big enough to take it. An eel with smooth skin that was spotted like a leopard, slid past. I changed my worm to a juicier-looking one.

Connor struck again.

Then finally I got one. Connor got one at the same time, and we re-baited, but Connor was quicker. He had another fish—outsmarted, outpulled—twisting on his line. I was catching up and I was getting better. Now I could feel the tiny tug that came up the line when they first bit.

Suddenly they stopped biting. For me anyway—Connor was still catching them. Pete had stopped fishing and was sitting on a log smoking a cigarette. I closed my eyes. *Come, fish, I command you. Come to my bait.* I opened my eyes just in time to see something big break the surface, brushing lily pads aside.

'Barra,' I cried and I yanked at the rod. The bait flew up into the fig tree.

'Ya see a barra, did ya?' said Pete, stubbing his cigarette out as he came over.

'It wasn't a barra,' scoffed Connor.

Had I seen a glint of silver? 'I definitely saw it,' I shot back, no longer sure what 'it' had been, only that it was big.

'You're just saying it 'cause I'm so far ahead of you,' said Connor.

'Are not,' I snapped back.

'Probably 'bout time we checked how many we've got,' said Pete. We crowded round the bucket. It was black with fish.

'Holy hell, there's tons,' I said.

'I can't even count them,' said Connor.

'Maybe we should put some back,' said Pete.

'Please can we keep them, Pete?' said Connor. 'We'll get worms for them every day, won't we Aaron. And we can have them there for barra bait whenever we need them. And I want to show Mum how many we got.'

'We could even breed them,' I added.

Pete shook his head. 'All right. Okay. But you two better look after them. And I mean every day.'

'Thanks, Pete,' I said.

Pete took off his shirt and put it over the bucket, which he then hoisted onto his shoulder and we were off, slower than we'd come, but now calling out to each other like pirates heading home with treasure.

As we drove I held the bucket between my knees, tilting it against the angle of the car to stop the water spilling.

'I can't believe we got so many. Can you, Connor?' I said. 'Mum's gunna freak.'

'They'll make good bait, them ones,' said Pete, but I could tell by the way he squinted at the road that his thoughts were somewhere else.

I said, 'Tell us about the secret spot, Pete.'

He glanced into the rear-view mirror, then with his eyes back on the road, he said, 'Well, it's on a farm but the farmer doesn't fish it. Pretty sure I'm the only one who does. It's a creek with dead trees in it, pretty shallow, lots of snags but tons of barra. Real big ones. Only problem is you have to keep an eye out for crocs: there's plenty of them too.'

I said, 'I can't wait to go.'

'Yeah we'll go,' said Pete, 'Us three. It'll be good.'

Connor, looking out the window, didn't say anything.

And in the silence, like a toothache, the rosary beads slid back into my head.

11

AARON AARONSON

WE PARKED UNDER the house, and Connor suddenly perked up. 'Right. Aaron, look sad,' he said. 'Pete, don't say anything.'

Mum was sitting on the back stairs with a magazine and a cigarette, which she quickly hid when she saw us. 'My boys are back. How did you go?'

Pete didn't say anything, I frowned and Connor sighed and said, 'Not too well.'

'Did you get anything?'

'We didn't get *much*,' said Connor.

'That's no good,' said Mum, as she ditched her magazine and came down the stairs. I had to turn away to hide my grin.

'So what's in the bucket?' she said.

'Well we did get *one* or two,' said Connor.

'Here, look,' I shrieked and ripped the shirt off the bucket.

'Holy hell,' shouted Mum, while Connor and I burst into gleeful laughter. 'How many are there?'

'A few,' said Pete.

'A few? Few hundred! What are you going to do with them all?' said Mum.

'Thought we could put them in the tub out by the chook pen,' said Pete.

So we lugged the bucket down behind the chook pen and in no time we had the old bathtub mucked out, freshly plugged and filled with water.

I heard Mum whisper, 'Why the hell did you get so many?'

'They were havin' a good time,' replied Pete hotly. 'There's plenty of mudcod in the world. Bet you'll be the first to eat all the barra we get with them.'

'I'll count them and you pour them in,' said Connor. 'But go slow.'

'We'll both count,' I replied.

They swam against the flow at first, but eventually a smallish one plopped into the tub.

'One,' Connor announced. 'Two. Three.'

They began to splash into the water.

'You're doing it too fast,' complained Connor.

'No, I'm not,' I said. 'Thirteen, fourteen.'

'I'm counting,' said Connor, and he grabbed at the bucket.

I shrugged him off. '*I'm* doing it.'

'Well, do it properly then,' said Connor.

'There's thirty-two,' I said when we'd finally watched the last of them into the tub.

'No, there's not, there's thirty-three,' said Connor.

'Either way,' Mum cut in, 'you're gunna have a job looking after them.'

We all looked down at the mudcod.

'I caught that one,' said Connor pointing to the biggest one.

'Good job, boys. Now come upstairs and you can tell me all about it.'

'I might stay down here,' I said.

'Suit yourself,' said Mum.

I stayed, waiting till the others were in the kitchen and I could steal away, return the rosary beads, and get back without anyone knowing I'd been gone.

In the meantime I watched the mudcod. They'd organised themselves into groups, with the bigger fish deeper. The biggest ones, right at the bottom of the tank, were the darkest colour, almost charcoal grey, and they had a dignity about them—they were the kings of the tub. All the fish seemed happy enough, apart from smallest one, the only one I was confident I'd caught, which was moving around near the surface like it was an unwanted kid.

'What's in there?'

I looked around; Byron's face was above the fence.

'How long have you been there?' I said.

'A while. I called out before, but you mustn't have heard me. I heard youse doing something.'

I couldn't see his chin. His head dipped and there was a crunching sound then he reappeared, chewing. 'What's in the tub?' he said.

'Some fish. We just caught 'em.'

'What sort?'

'Mudcod.'

He took hold of the top of the fence and I saw a Home Brand chocolate-chip muesli bar in his hand.

'Never heard of 'em. You gunna name 'em?'

It hadn't occurred to me. 'Yep. I'm gunna call that one down the bottom Connor Two, 'cause my brother Connor reckons he caught it and it's the biggest. And that's Pete Two 'cause he caught that one, and that little one's Aaron Aaronson 'cause *I* caught it. And that one there I'm gunna call Popeye 'cause one of his eyes is stuffed. Can you see 'em?'

'Not really.' He struggled to get higher up the fence, while I cornered a fish and lifted it out of the water.

'That's a rainfish,' said Byron.

'No, it's a mudcod.'

'I always called 'em rainfish. My Gran calls 'em rainfish.'

'Well Pete's a fisherman, and he says they're mudcod.'

'Who's Pete?'

'My mum's new friend.'

'Well, Gran grew up here all her life and she calls 'em rainfish.'

Something dawned on me. 'Is your gran an Aboriginal?'

'So?'

'Nothing.' That meant Byron was an Aboriginal too. He had brownish skin so that made sense.

I said, 'You don't eat these fish, do you?'

'No, you can't eat 'em. You want this?' He offered me the last bit of his muesli bar.

'Nah. Hey, my friend said to say thanks for the advice about the toy. He's gunna take it back right now. I'm gunna go help him.'

'Want me to come?'

'Maybe next time. My friend's a bit shy...'

'No worries. See ya.'

'See ya.' I was on my way through the yard on the way to the swamp, wondering whether I'd ever talked to an Aboriginal kid before. There were lots in Fingleton but only one or two at St Rita's, and none in my grade. We had some kids from Laos, some from Vietnam, and lots of Italian kids but they were born in Australia and were just like us, *us* being one of those things like who's cool and who isn't, who's tough and who isn't—it's one of those things everyone knows, even if they can't say why. I worried when I saw a bunch of Aboriginal kids coming down the street towards me. People said they stole things and got drunk. Mainly they didn't have much money. They ate witchetty grubs. Things I'd *seen* them do: swim at Polly's Creek, walk about the place, yell to each other across the street, win races at interschool sports. Things I hadn't seen them do: eat at restaurants, go to Scouts. *I should go over his house*, I thought. *But how will I get over the fence?* Weirdly, it didn't occur to me that I could just walk round and knock on his front door. *Of course they don't eat mudcod. What a dumb thing to ask.* I decided I'd name another fish Byron Bay, after Byron.

As I passed under the kitchen I heard a voice I

couldn't immediately place. *I'll just have a quick look before I go*, I thought, and crept up the back stairs and peeked through the bottom louvre of the kitchen window.

'That's a nice statue, Mrs Tate,' Damon was saying. He was talking about the Buddha on our sideboard. He was wearing a collared shirt, white shorts, and new-looking sneakers.

Mum's last name was Gorry not Tate, but she didn't correct him.

'Would you like something to drink, Damon?' she said in her good-manners voice.

'No, thank you, Mrs Tate.'

'How come you're so dressed up?' asked Connor.

'Me and Dad have just been to your school and met the principal. I'm going there after the holidays. I could be in your class.'

'What did you think? It's crap, right?' said Connor.

'Connor, don't use words like *crap*,' said Mum.

'I'm going to take Damon to see the fish,' said Connor, and before I knew it he and Damon were at the top of the stairs looking back at me.

'Were you spying on us?'

'No.'

With an annoyed sigh Connor brushed past me. I

followed them down the backyard to the tub.

'Aren't they cool?' Connor was saying. 'I got that one, the biggest one.'

'So interesting,' said Damon. 'Hey, why don't you go ask your mum if you can come over to my place?'

'Okay,' said Connor, and he ran off.

Damon squinted at me through his glasses. 'All good?'

'Yep,' I said, with a shrug and a smile that was so fake it hurt my face. He didn't reply, and the silence started to get to me so I said, 'All good.'

'You didn't go to the swamp did you? Yesterday?'

'What?' I said, trying to look confused. 'Nup.'

'I thought I saw someone there, that's all.'

'Lots of kids go guppy fishing and stuff there. I didn't go there,' I lied.

Damon nodded slowly. I couldn't tell if he believed me or not. 'Have you told anybody?'

'No.' I steeled myself. 'But did you read the paper? The police are going door to door checking people.'

'So? What are they going to do?'

I said, 'Take our fingerprints?'

He scoffed.

I forged ahead. 'I think we should take them back.'

'You can't. I've moved them.'

'What? Why?'

'They were too obvious where they were. Someone could've found them.' He sounded like he knew what I'd been planning. 'I put 'em somewhere way safer. I had some of the wine. It's pretty good. I'll give you some. Not yet, but. And you still can't tell *anyone*. In fact we should pretend we don't even know each other. Here he comes. What's your name again?' He said the last bit louder for Connor to hear.

'Aaron,' I said.

'She said I can go,' said Connor, 'but you have to stay here, Aaron.'

'Yeah, good. I don't want that baby tagging along,' said Damon, but he winked at me as he said it.

I went upstairs. Pete and Mum had disappeared somewhere. So I went down to Connor's room and, ignoring the sign on the door, let myself in. It was dark, as usual. *The Lord of the Rings* was on his bed. It was Mum's old copy, given to her by Dad when they were going out. It was so fat it was almost a cube. On the creased cardboard cover was a picture of two trees. Their branches intertwined, and little monsters were scurrying among their roots.

Connor had said I couldn't read it because I wouldn't understand it.

I opened it at random, looking for one of the battles, but mainly it was the hobbits walking around. Was there a battle near the start?

I tried again: 'I am deeply grateful,' said Frodo; 'but I wish you would tell me plainly what the Black Riders are. If I take your advice I may not see Gandalf for a long while, and I ought to know what is the danger that pursues me.'

Something made me stop and look around. A silence was building in the room, like a machine had been turned off and might at any minute start up again. The curtains were gently moving, as if they were breathing in and out. I imagined someone hiding behind them and though I knew it wasn't true I ran out, up to my room, and hid the book in my undies drawer.

After that I went back outside and found the soccer ball and began kicking it against the wall. Then I played out the Galactic Soccer Championship semi-final again, turning up the cheering of the crowd in my mind.

But as I dribbled the ball around the backyard, somehow I couldn't get Planet Earth to gel. Their passes were too hard and they didn't find their man, and Aaron Aaronson was the worst of the lot: he just could not score. Diego Chilly pulled one back, but when Mum called me up for lunch the score stood at 4–3, and the unthinkable had happened: Earth had been beaten, and Aaron Aaronson, for the first time in his brilliant career, had not been named Man of the Match.

12
PRISON

WIND WHIPPED THE branches of the mandarin trees in gusts, and with each gust a spray of rain shuddered the glass of my window and a sigh rose then sank to nothing. I dreamt I was in prison, and Mum was crying, which was the worst part—that and watching as she turned and left me in my cell. No more TV, no more soccer, just prison. No more fish and chips and ice cream. Just grey prison walls and barbwire, uniforms and rain, and porridge on trays. Like being stuck in class and knowing there'll never be a bell. Next I dreamt I was with Gandalf and the hobbits, running from the orcs. In front of us a river, crashing rapids, someone yelling something in some language that might have been Elvish, 'And now the fighting waxed furious on the fields of the Pelennor; and the din of arms rose upon high, with the crying of men and the neighing of horses.'

I rubbed my eyes. Opened them. Sighed. The trees outside my window were still, the wild weather of the night before was just a memory. Grade eight was one day closer. *And the rosary beads.* The guilt hit me. It began at my fingertips and spread. It sat heavy on my chest, like some big thing. Maybe an orc. What did orcs look like? I pictured big round yellow eyes, grey skin, a fat stomach, long, clawed fingers. And one was squatting on my chest, and there was nothing I could do but try to pretend it wasn't there.

The kitchen was deserted. As I climbed down the back stairs the loose planks shifted and bent under my weight. It was early; there was still dew on the grass. I crouched, yawning, by the rotten banana log and dug out a handful of worms. Then I made my way to the corner behind the chook pen, determined not to let any scaredy-catness put me off. But when I got there I found the way blocked—stretched in front of me, from the tip-most lemon leaf right to the wire of the chook pen, was a single thread of spider's web.

Where was the spider? I studied the leaves on the lemon tree, and had a sudden horrible thought that every leaf had a spider crouching behind it, from grain-of-sand-sized babies to hand-sized grandmothers. But that was just nonsense, and to prove it to myself I turned over the nearest leaf.

No spider.

Get a grip, Aaron.

I crawled under the web, careful not to break it because of some superstition I'd picked up somewhere—but also because why piss off a spider for no reason? Then I dropped the first worm into the tub and watched it sink, shaking granules of dirt off as it went. *Hurry up and eat it, fish*, I thought, but there it was, resting on the bottom.

I blinked. There were no fish in the tub. Actually, there was one, the smallest one, hovering in the corner.

I turned around. Mudcod were dotted all over the yard as if they'd sprouted from the ground like mushrooms or fallen in a meteor shower. Some were flapping. Most were still. How hadn't I noticed them before?

'The fish are out!' I yelled and I ran back to the house. 'The fish are out!'

'What?' came Connor's voice from his room, sounding like I'd woken him up.

'The fish are out.'

'What do you mean they're out?' He was at the foot

of the stairs, with that expression that said *you idiot* on his face.

'They're *out*. They must've jumped out.'

Pete appeared on the top step. 'Did you put a cover on 'em?'

'No.'

'Well that's why, then. Come on, let's put 'em back.'

'They'll be dead,' I said.

Pete was striding into the yard. 'I've seen 'em survive for ages out of water. Watch where you stand, they can get along a fair way.'

Connor was poking a toe at one near the clothesline. 'It moved!' he shouted.

'That's 'cause it's alive. Chuck him back in the tub,' said Pete.

One near my feet had wiggled itself between two clumps of grass so only its tail was showing, it was coated in dirt and twigs and its slime had turned black and hard. But when I picked it up it writhed sluggishly, and when I eased it into the tub it drifted to the bottom, then flicked its tail and swam about a bit looking totally fine.

With a fish in each hand and a lively one hugged to his chest, Pete broke the spider's web without noticing it and in one motion he deposited all three fish in the tub. As they slapped the water Pete was already looking for more.

I found one that was overrun with ants, and one whose eyes had been plucked out by a bird.

'Urrgh, that's disgusting,' said Mum who'd come down in her nightie, and was poking her toe at one. 'This'd be easier if you mowed the grass once in a while.' She made me pick up the live ones she found.

The most adventurous mudcod had made it halfway to the front gate. Pete later told me they travelled on dry land by using their fore-fins to shuffle along, just like the fish-looking things in the 'evolutionary parade' picture in our science book, who were the first creatures out of the primordial swamp, three or four stages before the chimps.

'So how many's that?' asked Mum eventually.

This time Connor and I were in agreement: 'Twenty alive ones and six dead ones.'

'And there were thirty-three before,' added Connor.

I said, 'Where are the others?'

'They'll turn up in the next day or so, when they start to smell,' said Pete. He disappeared under the house then came back holding three metal grills, which he placed over the bathtub.

'That oughta stop their little game,' he said.

Mum patted him on the back. 'Just in the nick of time,' she said.

Mum was at the stove cooking bacon and eggs while Pete was telling me and Connor about the time he'd upset a bucketful of mudcrabs that were as big as heads in a room full of drunk people, and everyone was barefoot and they were all screaming and jumping on chairs and tables, when from downstairs we heard Gran call, 'Are you home, Tracey?'

We looked at each other—Gran *never* came over.

'Careful, Gran,' called Mum, as we listened to the clunk of Gran's shoes on the bed planks. 'If she falls through it's your bloody fault,' Mum told Pete as she rushed out of the room to put her dressing gown on.

'Well,' said Gran, puffing, at the back door. She was wearing her green church dress and her high heels. She noticed Pete, who had retreated to the stove to turn off the bacon and eggs and she gave him a concerned smile like she thought he might be sick. 'Oh! Hello there,' she said. 'We haven't met. I'm Irene, the boys' grandmother.'

Mum returned just in time to say, 'This is Peter, Gran. My partner. I've been meaning to bring him round to your place.'

'Good to meet you, Gran,' said Pete from behind Mum. He reached over her and shook Gran's hand.

Suddenly the kitchen felt small.

'Well I'm pleased to meet *you*, Peter, and I hope I haven't come at a bad time.'

'No, Gran. You want a cuppa?' said Mum.

She did, so Pete put the kettle on while Gran smoothed Connor's and my hair like we were pet mice. 'Oh, it's good to see you boys, feels like a lifetime since I saw you pair,' she said. 'And you're not a local boy, are you, Peter. Are you planning to stay in Fingleton long?'

'Yep. Love it up this way. Love me fishing 'n' that,' he said.

'And have you been following this business at the church?' Gran sipped her tea and looked at me. 'I've never seen Father Lockhart in such a state. He stays in his room. I've been told he doesn't even come out to eat; the ladies put his tea on the floor outside his bedroom door. They say that when they go past sometimes they hear him sobbing. It's just too tragic. Because his father gave him those beads. And he hasn't given any instructions about the flowers for the Start of Term Mass. We're having to make it up as we go along.'

'It's kids,' said Mum, and Gran said, 'I don't doubt it,' and Mum said, 'Well it *was* kids. It said it in the paper.'

'I don't doubt it one minute.' Gran took another sip of her tea. 'Did I mention I need the car back? I'm going out to Rockhampton for a week to visit Beryl and the boys.'

'That'll be nice,' Mum said, but her smile said the opposite.

'Yes, always nice in that part of the world.' Gran sipped her tea and so did Mum.

Pete finished whatever he'd been doing at the sink and sat down with us, scraping his chair.

'Yes, it'll be good to see them,' said Gran. Then she moved her chair a little towards Mum and leaned in. And in a low whisper that we weren't supposed to hear but we all heard, she said, 'You know, I think Roger's there now. Hopefully I'll get to see him,' and she looked at Mum like she expected her to be happy about it.

Roger was Dad. Mum kept her mouth shut at the mention of his name. She'd never said it, but Connor and I knew that talking about him at our house was off limits.

Back at her normal volume Gran said, 'He's working as a chef. He always had a knack for cooking.

If you could have tried even his bacon and eggs, Peter. He just put so much of himself into it. Sounds to me like he's getting himself together again quite nicely. Did you boys get a chance to do a picture for him?'

I hadn't. Connor said he'd started one.

'Doesn't matter,' said Gran, 'How about you write him a little letter now?'

'Is he actually gunna call?' said Mum. 'This year?'

Gran looked taken aback by Mum's tone. With a little smile she said, 'Well he's been depressed, Tracey, as you know. It's a medical condition. He's working his way through things. I'll give the letters to him in person.'

'Why bother?' said Mum.

Gran folded her hands in her lap as if she'd won some sort of point.

Mum snorted, put her hands on the table and pushed herself up and left the kitchen.

Pete watched her go. The bedroom door slammed.

Gran was rummaging in her handbag. She took out a note pad and ripped two sheets from it, took out two pens and passed them to us. 'Go on, boys,' she said. 'Just write a little something for your dad. Whatever you want. I promise I won't read them. Peter, we might leave them to it for a bit, hey?'

She made her way to the back stairs and Pete followed. They stopped halfway down. I tapped the pen on my bottom lip. Connor had his head down and was writing already, but I couldn't stop thinking about what Gran had said about Father Lockhart. What if he stopped being a priest because he'd lost faith in humanity, and he hitchhiked to Townsville wearing jeans and a white T-shirt and checked into a seedy hotel and started fighting and swearing and became an alcoholic?

And then there was the Start of Term Mass, which in Fingleton was the fourth most important mass behind Christmas, Easter Sunday and Good Friday. Gran and her Catholic Ladies Group friends got in and mopped the church, arranged flowers, stitched banners saying 'Glory be', which they hung from the pillars, and then for the Mass they sat in the front row and turned around and glared at latecomers. Behind them sat the whole school including the teachers and even the tuckshop ladies. It was compulsory. Once Mum had crept in the back in her work clothes and stayed for a few minutes. That night she'd scoffed at it all, especially when the Catholic Ladies Group stood up just before the priest said, 'Please stand.' And she made me and Connor promise not to be taken in by it, and reminded us we only went there because it was the only decent school in town, and that we'd only been baptised to keep Gran happy and that she was going to look into having it reversed.

The Start of Term Mass always included Holy Communion—Father would put the wafer into each person's cupped hands, one by one. He'd see me right up close. And the Start of Term Mass was in the first week back at school. Only days away.

I heard Gran say to Pete, 'So that truck out the front is yours, is it Peter? I mean, do you own it outright?'

Pete agreed that it was his and that he owned it outright.

My page was still blank. It was easy for Connor. Connor was older when Dad had left but I was little, so I didn't remember much about him. There was him singing along to the radio while we drove—that had been in our first car, an old white Holden. And there were the things in the house that still had his smell—or was that just my imagination? And the pictures: him holding me when I was a baby, beaming behind his moustache like he couldn't believe it; him leaning against a wall with his arms crossed, smiling at the camera like the picture of a star in *TV Week* whose show I'd never seen.

And the letter he'd written me at Christmas in neat, strangely girly writing:

Dear Aaron. Hope you're having a wonderful Christmas. Your gran tells me you've been a good boy. That's the way, mate. Thinking about you and can't wait to see you. Love, your Dad.

Gran told Pete, 'You mustn't mind Tracey. She's a wonderful girl but she can get a bit stroppy. You have to tread on eggshells when it comes to certain subjects.'

'Gran, I don't know what to say,' I called out.

'Tell him what you've been up to. And say I love you.'

Dear Dad, How are you? I am fine, I wrote.

Once Mum had been preaching the evils of getting drunk and had mentioned the time Dad got drunk and someone broke his jaw, and she had to go get him from outside the pub.

'Don't you love the word "partner"?' said Gran to Pete. 'But it's good to see Tracey with a nice fella for a change, I must say. Of course what she does is her own business. After all, I'm not her mother. I'm the boys' father's mother.'

I wrote: *We went fishing and I caught lots of fish. It is holidays here. I went with my friend to the church.*

'Finished,' said Connor.

I looked down at what I'd written in astonishment and leaned so far forward on my chair that I nearly fell off. Connor was rereading the *Fingleton Gazette*, while outside Gran and Pete had gone quiet. The urge to write *and we stole some rosary beads* was overwhelming. Common sense told me not to. Obviously— Gran might see it. But she'd promised she wasn't going to read the letters.

And then, like I'd lost control of my hand, it began to write: *And we*—it was too late now—*took some rosary beads. What do you think I should do? Could you please give me some advice?* I finished with *love from Aaron,* then folded and folded it till it was almost the size of a postage stamp, thinking *Throw it away! Tell Gran you made a mistake and need to start again.* But when she came back I handed it to her. And, making a point of not looking at them, she put both letters in her handbag, which was one of those ones with gold clamps that give a satisfying snap when they shut. She patted Connor and me on the head and then took the car keys from Pete.

'Bye, Tracey,' she called. Then she said to Pete, 'Tell Tracey I'll be back in a week. And be extra nice to her for a bit. That goes for you boys as well.'

Run after her and get the letter back, I told myself.

But I didn't. I was in shock. I wondered what the hell stupid thing I was going to do next.

'She seems like a nice lady,' said Pete when she'd gone.

After a while Mum came back and began dishing out the bacon and eggs, which were cold by then. She gave Pete a dark look and banged down his plate like Gran coming over was his fault. He kind of smiled and shrugged. Then they started talking about other things, and gradually Mum forgot to be annoyed at him.

'Yeah, I was talking to Robbo last night,' said Pete. 'He reckons they need someone to do a spare-parts run to Sydney and back. Could be a regular thing. The first one's tomorrow.'

'On a Sunday?' said Mum.

'Yep, no rest days for truckies. It'll be bloody good if it comes off. It's been so bloody slow round here.'

Connor said, 'Have you been to Sydney before?'

'Yep. Hate it. Too many cars. Don't mind the harbour though.'

'Does it remind you of when you were a sea captain?' I asked.

'Nah, I just like the bridge. And the opera house.'

'Have you been to Sydney, Mum?' I asked.

'A hundred thousand horses couldn't drag me back there, with all the smog and the druggos. Nup, *this* is the best place in the world,' she said and she gestured out the window, and we all looked at the orange trees, the chook pen, the clothesline, the overcast sky. I couldn't work out what she was pointing at.

I said, 'Looks pretty boring to me.'

She gave an irritated sigh. 'I'm sick of doing the dishes. Connor, you and Aaron do them.'

'I'll wash,' said Connor.

I didn't argue.

Connor washed and I wiped. Droplets of rain spotted the window over the sink.

'It's spitting,' I said.

'Where were *you* Friday before last?' said Connor.

I coughed. 'What?'

Connor was watching me with a sly smile. 'I said where were you Friday before last? You know. The day the rosary beads got stolen.'

'Nowhere.'

'Yeah? So how come you looked so guilty when we were talking about it? You looked like you'd seen a ghost.'

'Shut up,' I said, louder than I meant to, 'I didn't take anything.'

Connor sniffed, 'Think I don't know that? As if you'd have the guts to do something as bad as that. I know who it was.'

I regained my composure. 'Who?'

'Stevie Harmison, of course. I found the coin thing right near his place. And don't forget he's got a big brother. He could have been the other boy.'

'Yeah,' I said. 'You're probably right.'

'Probably? Definitely. And I'm gunna catch him too.'

'How?'

'For me to know and you to find out,' he said and he smiled to himself as he rinsed the last plate.

'He's crazy, you know. You should just dob him in.'

'I don't want to do that till I'm positive. Anyway, he doesn't scare me. He's never scared me,' he said. Which I knew was true. Which was what made me uneasy.

After we'd put the dishes away I went downstairs to check on the fish. One was floating upside down on top of the water, but the rest seemed fine—especially the biggest ones, though there were only three of those now, hovering dark grey against the dark grey concrete of the tub. In fact they seemed relaxed, almost smug, and I felt like saying, *You know, you're miles from water, and there's nothing you can do about it.*

It was still spitting. In the long grass by the tank was a fish, one of the big ones, with clouded eyes and flies all over it. *Do we really need the grates? I wondered. Now they know that outside the bathtub is only dry land, will they really jump out again?* I got my answer when I took a grate off to scoop out the dead fish—another one jumped straight out and flipped and writhed like mad till I grabbed it and put it back.

The chooks never tried to escape. You could let them out, then put food in their pen and they'd run right back. Must have been something they liked about it. The chook pen's latch was off, and the wire door hung open. I went inside. Dried chook poo, dried-up orange peel and slivers of curled-up pecked-clean watermelon skin were scattered over the dirt floor. In the corner was a small corrugated-iron shed with wooden boxes and straw for the chooks to sleep in. The smell of chooks was everywhere, though they'd been gone six months. A python had eaten all but two of them, which we'd then given away. Afterwards Mum had sworn she'd never have another chook. I hooked my fingers in the chicken wire and peered out. *So this is what it's like to be in jail.* I shook the door, pretending it was locked.

I heard a noise behind me; something was in the corrugated-iron shed. *'Of course I'm not a black panther, ya idiot,'* it said in a sort of a hushing, dripping voice. *'And I'm not an orc. And no I'm not your guilty conscience come to life either.'*

'So what are you?' I said.

It didn't answer for a while.

Then when I thought it had gone it said, *'Anyway, you're not even guilty, are ya. You're just afraid of getting caught, that's all.'*

'Why won't you tell me what you are?'

'You can try to guess if you want. You'll never get it.'

Slowly, ever so slowly, I started to turn around. It was really dark inside the shed. Darker than it should have been. I peered into the darkness, and slowly my eyes started to get used to it, and I began, ever so slowly, to see a shape: the shape of the thing.

'Locked in, mate?'

I jumped. Pete was hurrying across the yard to let me out.

'Nah,' I said, embarrassed, and let go of the chicken wire. 'I was just pretending.'

Pete snorted. 'I used to do that sort of thing when I was a pup. You want to give me a hand with the truck?'

'All right,' I said.

And so I stood damply by as Pete hauled the truck's cab forward then stuck his top half into the engine, and tinkered and clinked while little spheres of rain stuck in the hairs on his legs.

'Pass the spanner, Aaron.'

'This one?'

With some difficulty he peered back at me. 'Nah, mate, other one.'

His transistor radio was on but he wasn't paying it any attention. Every now and then he swore quietly to himself.

What if I told him: *'Pete?' 'Yeah?' 'Me and another kid took the rosary beads.'* His eyes would go angry. *'How could you steal from a church? I'm telling your mum. And Father Lockhart. And I'm calling the police.'*

'Aaron, I just remembered, I was gunna tell ya something,' said Pete.

Before I could ask him what, I heard the low growl of an approaching engine; I looked up and saw a wide white bonnet, with the word *POLICE* across it, and two big faces at the windscreen. One of them was Ronny Landers' dad, perhaps the biggest man in Fingleton. He didn't look as friendly as when he'd given a Stranger Danger talk to my class.

'Gotta go to the toilet,' I said, and I hurried away, with my hands in my pockets and my head down.

I ran to the backyard and climbed into the leafy branches of the avocado tree.

13

ANOTHER SECRET

AS I CLIMBED up to my branch in the avocado tree I knocked something off. It was *Aboriginal Tales of the Far North*. It fell open on the grass below on page fifty-two. Because I'd put a bookmark there—the prayer card we'd taken from the church. Now it was just lying there for Connor or the police or anyone to find.

Mum's we've-got-guests voice floated from the kitchen, and a man's voice that could only have been a policeman's because of how deep it was. And here I was with the biggest clue in the world. I jumped down, grabbed the card and sprinted under the house.

Mum yelled, 'Connor!' just as I was in front of his door. I heard him sigh and throw his book down and yell, 'Coming!'

I ran round to the front of the house. The police

car was parked in our driveway. And Pete was still working on the truck. I darted up the front stairs, my heart racing a million miles an hour, then crept into my room. *Made it!* I breathed a sigh of relief.

I could hear Connor in the kitchen. What was he doing? Wowing them with his 'Possibles' and 'Probables' lists?

I looked at the picture on the back of the card again. There was definitely something weird about the angel's smile. It seemed to say she wasn't against the idea of the kids in the picture falling down the cliff, that she thought it might be kind of funny if they did.

'Aaron.'

I jumped.

Mum was at my door, coffee in hand. 'What are you up to?'

'Nothing,' I said as I slipped the card into my undies drawer.

'The police are here. They want to talk to you. Come to the kitchen.'

I followed her, and there, sitting at the kitchen table, with a cup of tea in front of him, was Mr Landers in his police uniform. He was bony faced, with bushy browny-blond eyebrows. He'd taken off his cap and balanced it on his knee. His thin hair was sweaty and flattened and there was a red band across his forehead where the cap had been.

He said, 'G'day mate. You're Connor, right?'

'He's Aaron. The big one's Connor,' said Mum.

'How could I forget? Sorry, Trace.' He smiled at me briefly, picked up a pad and pen and said, 'Aaron. You don't know anything about this church business, do you, Aaron?'

I shook my head.

'Answer, Aaron,' said Mum.

'No,' I said.

'It's okay, mate, nothing to be nervous about.'

'Nope.'

He looked me in the eyes. He was frowning. I couldn't say *no* again, that would be three times which meant you were lying. I'd heard that somewhere.

He wrote something on his pad and said, 'Take a seat, mate.'

I sat down.

He put the pad in front of me. 'I want you to write some things down, okay? Ready? *Now is the time for all good men to come to the aid of their party.*' He waited while I wrote it down. 'Now write *The quick brown fox jumps over the lazy dog.* Now write, *Every Tom, Dick and Harry in town will be there.* Okay, now just write down your name and address and that's that.'

When I'd finished he picked up the pad and studied it. He nodded to himself; then he squinted at me and said, 'And you don't know anything about it? No one's said anything to you about it?'

I shook my head.

He nodded again, flipped the pad closed. He said 'Thanks, mate.' Then he turned to Mum. 'Routine stuff. But I might just leave my card, Trace, in case anyone remembers anything.'

'So you're just going door to door, hey?' said Mum.

'At this stage. Working our way out round the streets around the church, probably just to the end of Shoe Street.'

'You gunna find 'em, you reckon?' said Mum.

Mr Landers stood up and took his cup to the sink but didn't wash it. 'Got a good chance. You tend to in these types of things. Something gives, you know?' He glanced at me. 'Anyway, I'm gunna chip away at it. No rush. See what turns up.'

'Good luck,' said Mum. 'Don't let the little bastards get away with it.'

He nodded. 'I'm quietly confident. Oh, yeah, I forgot.' He reached into his pocket and pulled out mum's necklace. 'I found this out the front of your place. Is it yours?'

Mum took it with a frown. 'That's weird,' she said. 'Yeah it's mine all right. Thanks for that.' She put it on the sideboard in the bowl we kept keys and odds and ends in.

'No worries,' said Mr Landers. 'All right, see ya, Trace. See ya, Aaron.'

Mum said, 'See ya, Paul.' She still had her coffee mug in her hand; she hadn't taken a sip since Mr Landers had come. When he'd left she turned to me and said, 'Why was my necklace out on the street, Aaron?'

I shrugged.

'Aaron?' She watched me, waiting for an answer.

'I didn't put it there.'

'I wonder who it was, then,' she said and she sighed. 'And you don't know anything about this church stuff, right? *Right?*'

I shook my head.

'Well then, why were you being so weird?'

'Dunno.'

She looked unsatisfied. 'Well next time someone asks you a question, *especially* a policeman, bloody answer them, for God's sake. All right? Policemen are just normal people. There's nothing to be frightened about.'

'Yes, Mum. Sorry, Mum,' I said.

But she wasn't finished. 'And there's nothing you want to tell me? You know you can tell me anything, right?'

'There's nothing, Mum.'

She had her back to the sink, leaning on it. 'Well don't scare me like that. You're supposed to be the level-headed one. You're supposed to be the one I don't have to worry about.'

'Sorry, Mum.'

She sighed. 'All right, off ya go.'

I ran to my room and lay on my bed with my pillow over my head and stayed there, holding my breath as long as I could, over and over. Lying to the police was a criminal offence, I was pretty sure. And it felt terrible to lie to Mum, but what option did I have? The level-headed one? Was she nuts? That she could think of me that way somehow made me feel even more lonely.

I stayed in my room till Mum called us for lunch. It was spaghetti on toast.

'Where'd you get off to?' Pete asked.

I shrugged.

'What did you say to the policeman?' I whispered to Connor.

'Nothing. He just got me to write some stuff down, for some reason.'

'Anyway, you two, I've got an announcement,' said Pete, looking at Mum. 'Your Mum and me have been talking, and she told me that you two can keep a secret. That true?'

'Definitely,' said Connor, 'I can assure you.'

'I can,' I said with less conviction.

'That's what I thought. Well then, after I do this next job tomorrow, I'm going to take you two to me secret fishing spot, but—'

Connor cheered.

'But, you have to promise you won't tell anyone where it is. Do you promise?'

'One hundred per cent,' said Connor, and I promised as well.

'Good. Now, they'll need a good pair of shoes, Trace, 'cause there's a bit of walking. And we'll need sunscreen.'

'I made up some names for the fish,' I said.

'Don't get too attached to 'em, mate. That's our bait.'

'We can keep a few of them, though, can't we?'

'Course, mate. Now let's see, youse'll need your hats...'

'I don't feel like any more lunch,' I said.

'You haven't had any,' said Mum.

'I'm not hungry,' I said. And I wasn't. 'Can I leave the table?'

'Go on then.'

I tipped my toast into the scrap container by the sink, and then went back to my room. I wasn't sure I could keep a secret. The biggest one I'd ever had felt like it was going to burst out of me at any minute.

14
FINGERPRINTS

WHILE WE ATE dinner the rain bore in from the sea. 'Here we go,' said Mum, and we all stopped chewing to listen. First came a single drop—*slap*—on our metal roof, then a short sharp machine gun *ratatatatat*, then a roar like being inside a giant shell. We had to yell to hear each other, and after dinner we had to turn the TV right up. It was cosy on the couch with Mum, just the pale blue of the television lighting the room, as outside the storm railed around the house.

'Good rain,' said Pete from the big chair.

Mum shrugged. 'About average,' she said.

'It's always like this, *hey* Mum,' said Connor.

'Southerners, thinking they know about rain,' said Mum.

'I've been here two years,' scoffed Pete.

'That's right,' she said. 'You just got here.'

The Cannonball Run was on. Halfway through Pete disappeared out to the back stairs for a cigarette. The smoke drifted into the kitchen; I gave a little cough on my way to the toilet in the ad break, but he didn't notice me. He just kept staring out at the rain. Mum let us watch the whole movie so I ended up going to bed at eleven. Still the rain kept on, cooling the air, filling my head. I went to sleep feeling like I was wrapped in cottonwool.

When I woke up I kept my eyes closed. I lay perfectly still with my arms and legs frozen, my breathing slow, because to move even an inch would start the day and restart my rosary-beads nightmare. If I stayed just as I was maybe I could keep everything frozen in the moment. Maybe the whole day even.

It was still raining. Instinctively I knew it had rained all night. And there was another sound too apart from the rain on the roof. It was a higher-pitched plip-plopping which I decided, after some thought, was the sound of rain falling on water.

The new sound teased me from bed.

There was a puddle on the floor outside my room, and I felt a drip on my head, but looking up I couldn't see the leak through the spiderweb across the shadowy ceiling.

The dinner things were still on the kitchen table. Ants tracked along the plastic lace tablecloth, circling the edges of smudges of gravy and fat on the plates. *Whoever was here, looks like they left in a hurry*, a policeman would've said. The morning twilight made everything seem unreal. I looked through the back window at our yard. It was underwater: from the back fence, the bases of the orange trees, to the clothesline, and right up to the house.

And it was still raining hard, making a mist over the surface of the water.

I ran downstairs. The water was ankle deep, clear and cool. It had even spread onto the concrete under our house. I heard sploshing; Connor was up.

'Is it in your room?' I called.

'Nearly,' said Connor. 'It's astounding. It's bloody astounding.'

We ran through the curtain of water that overflowed from the roof gutter, then ran back through it, and we were soaked. We jumped and splashed, whooping and shouting.

Suddenly Connor yelled, 'There's something there.' And he pointed out into the yard. A dark shape was moving against the green of the submerged grass near the clothesline, making a small bow wave on the surface of the water. 'What the hell is that?'

It marooned itself, had to wriggle free.

One of the gratings was leaning against the side of the bathtub.

'It's a mudcod,' I said.

Connor ran out after it and I climbed the stairs and yelled, 'Mum, Pete, come and look!'

Pete appeared at the door, took in the scene, and said, 'Bloody hell.'

There were mudcod milling under the banana trees, mudcod in twos and threes in front of the chook pen, and in the dripping shade of the orange trees. And who knew how many were lurking around the bathtub where the water was deeper, and a grey colour. There weren't many near the base of the clothesline where there was only a couple of centimetres of water. One or two of the mudcod, like the one Connor was chasing, were urgently zigzagging across the grass, but most of them hovered where they were, like the yard was *their* place and *we* were the trespassers.

I turned to Pete. 'What do we do now?'

'Just got to catch them,' he said.

'Okay.' I sprang at the nearest mudcod but it slipped through my hands like soap and made a dash for the orange trees. I intercepted it, sprang at it again and missed it again. But on the third attempt I managed to trap it with my forearms against my stomach. Hunched over, I staggered to the bathtub, which was full to the lip, dropped it in and put the grates back on.

'Good work, mate,' said Pete. He was after one. His long legs were pumping. He darted down and came up triumphant with a fish in his hand. Mum helped out, using a bucket—a much better way. Connor caught one with an ice-cream container. I stalked up behind one near the chook pen, eased my hands round its soft belly and lifted it without it seeming to notice or care.

After ten minutes the remaining mudcod were mainly bunched under the banana trees, shadowy shapes moving slowly. I took Mum's bucket, and Pete, Connor and I moved on them together, scattering them as we pounced but catching two as well.

'There's one under the house,' yelled Mum.

We ran to help her.

'Don't jump about so much,' said Connor. 'You're stirring up the dirt.'

Mum said, 'Don't let it get to the pot plants.'

But it was already there. We began picking up the pots one by one. There was a swish of a tail. It was the big one—Connor Two.

'He's coming to you,' I shouted to Connor.

We all lunged at it. I got Connor's foot, and Pete got the mudcod.

After Pete put Connor Two back we tallied the ones we had caught. I was starting to shiver.

'There's only nine,' said Connor. 'The rest must be around here somewhere.'

Connor and I kept up the hunt while Mum and Pete had a shower, but we didn't catch any more. I checked around the side of the house where the water got shallower and became a stream that flowed down our driveway to the foaming brown torrent of the gutter. I could picture some of the mudcod flicking and slithering their way to it—after all I'd seen how far they could go on dry land. From the gutter it was a quick ride to the stormwater drain at the end of our block, from there to be sucked down to the flood gates that lead to the river, and then to the sea. Some might even have managed to find the mouth of their own creek and returned to their little pond in the rainforest. I watched the gutter water running past, and hoped that they had.

'You think the whole town might flood, Mum?' I asked while we had our breakfast and listened to the rain thundering on the roof. Pete was in his truck driver's singlet with his bilum slung over the back of his chair.

'Hey, school might even be cancelled tomorrow,' said Connor. 'That'd be *so* cool.'

But I knew he couldn't wait for school to start.

'You'll be going to school even if you have to swim,' said Mum.

Connor turned to Pete. 'Where do you think the other mudcod went?' he asked.

'Be down round the bananas still, I reckon. It's pretty deep back there.'

I said, 'I reckon some got into the gutter and swam back to their pond.'

Connor scoffed.

'Stranger things have happened,' said Pete.

The phone rang. I beat Connor to it and then passed it to Pete, who gulped a quick mouthful of coffee before answering: 'Peter…Yep…Yep…Nup. No worries. Yep, yep…No, she's right. Good one. Righto.'

He hung up. 'Highway's flooded at Feluga.'

That's where it always flooded—cutting off the whole top bit of Australia. 'Robbo reckons there's a jam in front of it a K long. Looks like I won't be going on that job unless something changes pretty quick smart.' He smiled over his mug at Mum.

'So are they *postponing* it?' she said.

'Dunno. Said he'll ring back, but I reckon it'll be a few days at least. *Just average rain*, she says.'

Mum leaned over his chair and hugged him from behind. 'Oh, Pete.'

Pete gently wriggled away. 'It's all right. Bloody hell, it's *good*. I get to keep me holiday going,' he said and he leaned back on his chair and put his arms behind his head like he was on a hammock slung between two coconut trees. 'Might have to make the next one a beer.'

'I'm gunna go and see how Damon's place is,' said Connor, and I said, 'Me too.'

'No!' Connor said, turning to Mum. 'Tell Aaron he can't come.'

Mum, still wrapped around Pete's shoulders, sighed. 'Let him go along, Connor. He won't get in the way. Will you, Aaron?'

'I promise I won't,' I said.

'He will, Mum. He always does.'

'Off you go and play nicely together. And take the umbrella.'

Connor was fuming. He banged the umbrella tip on each one of the front stairs on his way down before unfurling it into the face of the pelting rain.

I followed him. Out on the footpath I said, 'It's raining. You have to let me under.'

He stopped, turned round deliberately and said, 'F. Off.'

'I'm gunna tell Mum you swore.'

He didn't answer, just kept walking, and I kept following.

The stormwater drain at the corner was working hard to suck in all the water from the gutter. It gave out a hollow crashing sound like there was a Niagara Falls deep underground. It made me shudder: the thought of getting sucked down there.

Connor stopped. He picked up a rock from the footpath and cocked his arm as if he was going to throw it at me. 'Go home. Go find your own friends.'

'If you chuck that I'm telling.' *You'd miss anyway*, I added to myself. I wasn't going to be put off *that* easily.

On Shoe Street, out the front of the Harmisons' house, we came across Damon under an umbrella, watching none other than a soaking wet Stevie Harmison racing paddle-pop sticks along the gutter. Stevie was calf-deep in the gutter, but he was still almost as tall as Damon who was standing on the footpath.

'How ya going, Connor?' said Damon, without

looking at me. 'Check out the rain last night. The weather round here's nuts.'

Stevie was watching us, smiling to himself like bullies do, with that wolf smile. The rain had made his blond hair into ringlets on his forehead and he had a streak of mud on his face that looked like it had been added by a make-up artist. His bike lay by the footpath.

'Hey, Damon,' said Connor uncertainly. He'd stopped a way off, and I was further back still.

Damon, still ignoring me, said, 'Me 'n' Stevie are racing paddle-pop sticks.'

Stevie stepped out of the gutter and up to Connor and said, 'Hey Minnie Mouse, good ta see ya, mate.' And he shook Connor's hand with mock respect. To Damon he said, 'People call this one Minnie Mouse and that one Mickey.'

No one had ever called us that.

Damon looked from Stevie to Connor.

'G'day, Stevie,' said Connor. 'What have you been up to lately?'

'What have I been up to? None of your ugly loser business is what I've been up to.'

'Interesting. Have you been round the primary school lately? And is that a new bike? Very nice.

Come into some money, maybe?'

Stevie shook his head, took a step back, baffled, trying to find a thread of meaning in Connor's words. 'Umm. No, it's not a new bike. It's like a year old. You are honestly weird, you know that? Honestly not right in the head.'

'Huh,' said Connor with an enigmatic smile, and he turned to Damon. 'You got much water at your place, Damon?'

'You *could* say that. The backyard's totally flooded.' He pointed his chin in my direction. 'How come you brought *him* along?' he said.

Connor looked round at me. 'I didn't. Go home, Aaron.'

I was trying to signal to Damon that I had something to tell him.

'No, you gotta do it like this,' said Damon. 'FUCK OFF!' he yelled at me. 'And then if he doesn't go you chuck something at him.' He made a show of looking around for something to throw.

Stevie, of course, thought it was hilarious. Damon had found a rock and was brandishing it in one hand and holding his umbrella in the other, advancing on me, with his piggy eyes wide behind his glasses.

'Aaron,' said Connor, in a warning tone of voice,

but I had already started for home. They had another think coming if they thought I was going to cry.

As I turned the corner I heard a yell, and footsteps behind me. It was Damon.

'Now I got ya,' he called for the benefit of the others. He tossed the rock aside, grabbed my shoulder, then hissed, 'What the hell are you doing? We're supposed to not know each other, remember?'

'What are *you* doing?' I shot back, 'Why'd you nearly chuck a rock at me? And why'd you say *fuck off* like that?'

He pulled me close up to his face and whispered excitedly, 'What was I supposed to say? *Hi Aaron, old buddy, old pal*? Do you *want* us to get caught or something? Tell me what you wanted to tell me. Quickly.'

I took a deep breath. 'The police came to my place. They made me and Connor write stuff down. They're going round checking everyone's handwriting. They're gunna go to the end of Shoe Street. To your place.'

'Why?'

'You wrote *dickhead* on the pad, remember? They're gunna catch us. You have to give the beads back.'

'Why?' he said, but he was thinking, biting his lower lip as raindrops popped hollowly on the umbrella and rolled off onto my back. He let go of my shoulder.

I couldn't stop the crack in my voice when I said, "Cause they'll catch us.'

Damon took his glasses off, wiped them, put them on again, and then said, 'I'll just write with my left hand. My uncle's a cop, and *he* told *me* that if you get caught for something, if you don't admit it they can't prove it, so you'll get off. So if they catch you *don't* say it was us. You can say it was someone else, or even just say nothing, but don't admit it. All right?'

'But will you put them back? *Please.*'

'They'll have our fingerprints on them.' He was right. We were stuck.

'I'll think about it,' he said at last, 'but you have to promise *not* to come round my house or try to hang around me, okay? Not till it's all over.'

'But...' But I couldn't think of anything else to say.

'I'll see you soon,' he said. Then he shoved me towards home and added loudly, 'And don't come back,' as Connor had peeked round the corner, looking relieved to see me not beaten to a pulp.

As they left I heard Connor say, 'Why are you hanging around *him*?' He meant Stevie Harmison. 'He's the one who broke into the church.'

I pondered what Damon had said as I walked home and as I waded through our backyard watched by a mudcod hovering in the water in front of the chook pen. The yard seemed foreign, like the tidal lagoon of an island I was shipwrecked on. I imagined coral in the shallows, a giant clam and, lurking in the deep, a shark. I climbed the avocado tree—going carefully because the trunk's skin of lichen and moss had been softened and sliprified by the rain.

Eventually I made it to the fork in the branches and I clung there like a stranded possum, feeling as sorry for myself as I ever had in my life.

You could say someone else did it. Could that work? I could say Connor did it. I pictured the police arresting Connor, the scared look on his face, him crying like a baby, pee all down his leg, probably, and as I thought all this a cold chill swept over me and I shivered.

'Wotcha doing up there?'

An umbrella swayed above the back fence, under it Byron's face was just visible through the rain, his eyes wide. 'Holy hell, your place's almost as bad as mine.'

I climbed down from the tree and splashed over to the corner behind the chook pen, stopping with the water at my knees. No spiderweb. Where did spiders go when it rained?

'Is your place flooded too?' I asked.

'Yeah, it's right under my house.'

I jumped up but I couldn't see over the fence. 'It's under my house too a bit,' I said.

Byron stretched his neck to see under my house, but he couldn't. He scratched his nose and made a clicking noise with his tongue. 'Hey, how are the fish?'

'They got out. We got some of 'em back, though.'

'I asked my gran how come they're called rainfish. She said they're always called that. She says you're not supposed to catch 'em.'

That was when it clicked. *Of course*—the rainfish from *Aboriginal Tales of the Far North*. Why hadn't I thought of that before?

I said, 'I know people who catch them all the time.'

'That's just what she said, anyway.'

An idea struck me, 'Did *you* let them out?'

'No. Hey, did your friend take that toy he stole back to the shop?'

Out of nowhere, I felt myself getting angry. 'That's dumb about them being rainfish, no one calls them that, they're just mudcod.'

Byron frowned. I held his gaze. Finally, he said, 'Dumb, hey? Want a smack in the head, ya dumb fuck?' He disappeared. Moments later a rock flew from behind the fence and landed near me with a splash. My third near miss with a rock that morning.

'Good one,' I called sarcastically but got no answer.

'Dickhead,' I yelled. But by then I knew he was gone.

I went upstairs. Mum and Pete were in the kitchen drinking beer and listening to the radio.

I had a shower, then went and sat out on the front veranda. I thought about what Byron had said. Could all this rain be because we'd caught some rainfish? 'Of course not,' I said out loud to the street that was grey from all the rain that was still pouring down. *Primary-school stuff.* I went inside and watched TV.

Later that afternoon when Connor came back, Mum roped me into helping him take his things upstairs. Most of it we put in the corner of the lounge room where our presents were piled every Christmas. I wasn't talking to Connor, and he wasn't talking to me.

'Has anyone seen *The Lord of the Rings*?' he asked.

I just smiled to myself.

Pete helped us drag Connor's bed up the stairs—we left it on its side in the hall next to a bucket that was catching water from the leak in the roof.

That night was the first time I'd ever paid attention to the weather report. They mentioned the highway being out. They even mentioned Fingleton by name. 'Fingleton: more showers expected.'

'So it's going to keep raining, is it, Mum?' I asked.

'Weather people are wrong as much as they're right. But we've got everything out from downstairs 'cept the Datsun, and it's not going anywhere. Maybe you should think about moving the truck though, Pete. It's pretty low where it is.'

Pete had been drinking all day. He had a lazy grin on his face.

'She'll be right,' he said.

Mum looked at him for a while, then gave her trademark irritated sigh. 'And has anyone seen my necklace? The one the police found? I put it in the sideboard bowl and now it's gone again.'

No one said anything. Connor just kept watching TV like he hadn't heard.

'So it grew legs and ran off, ay?' said Mum, 'There's certainly some unusual stuff happening around here.'

That night Connor slept on the top bunk. 'It's not bad being back in the old bunk,' he said.

I didn't reply.

'You're probably wondering why I didn't tell the police about Stevie, right? It's 'cause I need more proof. I'm going to get it too. I'd love to check his house, but his mum's home all the time. Must be something wrong with her.' He yawned. 'I set a trap for him today while you and Damon were talking about whatever it was you were talking about. He's my only other suspect now by the way.'

I couldn't help myself. 'Who?'

'Damon. I mean I can't see Damon doing that—he's my best friend—but logically it's got to be one of those two.' He made a stretching noise, and after a while he said, 'I hope school's flooded out tomorrow.'

I heard him rummaging. 'Look what I found,' he said, and dangled the miniature Rubik's cube by its keyring from his bed. 'I wonder how it got up here?'

'Beats me,' I said.

'Yep, definitely hope there's no school tomorrow.'

I didn't say anything.

He was quiet for a while. Then he said, 'Night, Aaron.'

The squeak of Connor twisting his Rubik's cube, mixed with the shushing of rain on the roof, began to make me sleepy. Of course the rainfish story wasn't real. But imagine if it was. In the story they'd had to climb the highest tree. I thought about me and Connor and Mum and Pete in the top branches of the fig tree at the oval, which was the biggest tree I knew, and water all around. And there was a bunyip. And what made the rain stop, in the end? Did the boy jump in the water, or did someone push him? I couldn't remember.

Probably it would stop raining soon and then we'd have to go to school, which would be just my luck.

15

THE NECKLACE TRAP

I OPENED MY eyes. It was pitch black. From the top bunk came the sound of Connor's delicate snoring. The rain had intensified, it thrashed at the house, angry, determined. And in my half sleep I thought, *It hates us. It wants to get in and wash everything away. It's going to rip the roof off and smash the windows. It's never going to stop.*

Connor was shaking me. It was morning. 'Aaron, get up. Come and see,' he said.

We ran to the kitchen, joining Mum who was staring out the louvres. A single glance told me there'd be no school that day: the water had turned from clear to coffee coloured, and it had risen to the lower branches of the mandarin trees; their trunks were submerged so they looked like shrubs on a flat brown desert. The orange and avocado trees were half under too, and the clothesline. Towards the chook pen Mrs Melchiori's fence disappeared completely. Only the topmost leaves of the lemon tree were showing. The bathtub was invisible.

The bottom three planks Pete had put down as stairs had come off and were floating in the yard, which made it feel like the house was a houseboat off its anchor and drifting and we were along for the ride to who knew where. And it was still raining. Like I'd known it would be.

The side of the house and the driveway were under as well. I ran out the front—all along the street people were out on their verandas. The road was underwater. A motorboat putted past. The man at the outboard was enjoying the attention he was getting; he even waved at one point, seemingly to no one in particular. His passengers, a woman and a little boy in life jackets, gripped the sides of the boat like they thought it might tip at any moment.

Pete's truck was in above its wheels. The boat's bow wave pushed water up to its doors.

Mum was behind me. 'Pete, the truck,' she called.

Pete came out of the bedroom, still half asleep and wearing only his boxers.

'Oh no,' he said, with his arms by his sides. 'Bloody hell,' he said louder.

'It might be okay,' said Mum. 'Go see if you can start it.'

Pete got the keys and rushed down the front stairs. He waded through the gutter, where the water was up to his waist. When he got to the truck he opened the passenger door and shimmied over to the driver's seat.

We waited for the sound of the engine starting.

Nothing.

After a while he got out and came back up. His sopping boxers clung to his thin legs as he stood there on the front porch. He looked skinny; I hadn't realised how skinny he was.

He said, 'I'll ring Robbo, see if he can tow it out.'

But Robbo said he couldn't do anything till the water came down.

'Fridge is off,' said Mum. 'Power must be out.'

We ate breakfast listening to at least two choppers hovering above us. After that Pete set up a little diesel generator we kept in the kitchen cupboard for cyclones, which often took out the power, and we moved to the lounge room to see if the flood had made the morning TV news.

We were the second story. The newsreader lady

said, 'Torrential rain has closed roads throughout the Far North of Queensland and inundated some two hundred homes in the coastal town of Fingleton. The water has also cut power and other utilities to homes and businesses and forced the evacuation of hundreds. For more we're joined by Sarah Hutchinson who is in Fingleton. Sarah, what more can you tell us?'

They cut to a young woman in a yellow raincoat.

Connor said, 'She's on Edith Street!' which was only a few blocks away. She was in front of Sam's Pies, which had a wall of sandbags across its front door.

Sarah Hutchinson said, 'The State Government has today declared Fingleton a disaster zone after an unprecedented downpour last night caused extraordinary flooding in this sleepy coastal town. The town recorded a whopping six hundred millimetres in about six hours last night, which to put it into perspective is about a fifth of the annual rainfall. The SES has been kept busy rescuing people from their cars and evacuating residents to higher ground. A short time ago I spoke to some locals about their experiences.'

They cut to footage from a helicopter: the low-lying parts of town, like our part, were all underwater, while higher parts like near the church and the school had been spared. The streets were brown with floodwater;

some roofs had people on them.

'There's us,' said Connor. 'I saw our house.'

Sarah Hutchinson's voice came back on. 'Fingleton is known for its high rainfall, but few have seen anything like the current flood.'

An old man in a cowboy hat and a singlet spoke into a microphone, 'Fingleton's had a few floods. The big one was 1962. But I've never seen it come up so quick.'

A man in an orange council-worker shirt said, 'Yeah, I had water all through me house, it come up in about twenty minutes. Reckon I lost about ninety per cent of me stuff. TV, fridge, all me food. I've got two kids, they're in town. But I'm staying, see how bad it gets.'

They showed St Rita's High School, with people going in and out carrying boxes. They showed a classroom with mattresses and blankets, people playing cards, kids running around.

'Obviously not going to be any school for a while,' said Mum.

Sarah Hutchinson was saying, 'Evacuation centres have been set up in local schools and the shire hall. Many people have been evacuated, some by boat, some airlifted by helicopter, and are settling in for the night.'

The newsreader said, 'Sarah, how busy does the SES think those evacuation centres will be tonight?'

Sarah was back at the pie shop. 'Very busy indeed. Hundreds of residents have been forced to flee their homes. And the bad news is, as you can see, it's still raining here, and forecasters are warning it's set to continue. And with an expected king tide in the early hours of tomorrow morning, there appears to be no reprieve in sight.'

'Thank you, Sarah,' said the newsreader. 'The Queensland premier is due to make a statement later this morning and is expected to travel to Fingleton today to survey the damage.'

'Thanks be to God,' said Mum sarcastically.

I left the others watching TV and went back out to the front veranda. Some kids were on the street in raincoats splashing each other and some other kids were in a blow-up raft being pulled and pushed by more kids I didn't know. Everyone was yelling and wet and everyone was happy and carefree.

Karen, who worked with Mum at the pub and lived in a unit on top of the hill, waded up to our house. 'Aaron, can you go get your mum for me?'

When Mum appeared Karen started to laugh, 'Tracey, oh my God, *look* at *your* place.'

'Pretty impressive, hey?' Mum replied. 'You want to come up?'

'Can you come out?'

So Mum waded out to Karen and soon they were deep in conversation.

'Aaron,' called Mum from the road. 'I'm going with Karen to check on Gran's place. You and Connor stay here, all right? Peter's in charge so do what he tells you. I won't be long.'

'Okay,' I said and I watched them splash off together.

Inside, Pete and Connor were watching an Aussie Rules game on TV. Pete had a beer. I sat down beside him and waited till the ad break. 'Mum's gone out with Karen. She said she won't be long.'

'U-huh,' said Pete, eyes on the game.

'Pete,' said Connor. 'I'm gunna go visit my friend Damon, okay?'

Pete sat up a bit. 'Where's he live?'

'Just up the road.'

'How you gunna get there?' he asked suspiciously.

'Walk. I can walk there. It's close. And if the water's too high I'll come straight back.'

'I'm going too,' I said.

'Aaron,' said Connor, shaking his head.

'He's my friend too,' I said quietly.

Connor scoffed.

'Now, Connor,' said Pete, glancing at me, 'You have to include your brother. Either take Aaron or you're not going. Simple as that, mate.'

'All right,' sighed Connor. 'Come on then.'

The kids and their raft were off in the distance, but the street was still rowdy because the people two houses down from us had pulled their couch out onto their veranda and were drinking beer and playing rock music.

A man in a shiny green raincoat—it was probably his car parked on the rise near the school where the water hadn't reached—was taking photos of Pete's truck, crouching, trying out different angles. Pete had followed us onto the veranda and was leaning against the door, beer in hand, watching the camera man. He had a look on his face like he was contemplating telling the man to piss off.

The water was cold and dirty. I was in up to my ankles. On the bottom front step and I couldn't see my feet. Connor was knee deep where he waited by the gate post that still had Pete's mug on it from the day he'd driven off in such a hurry. I stepped out, and found the ground not exactly where I'd thought it would be, as if it'd pulled away slightly at the last minute.

The yards of the houses across the street were all under as well. In the distance to the left a procession of people were carrying chairs and bags of clothes above their heads. To our right, half the high-school oval was underwater.

I eased my way towards the gutter and tried the depth there. Then I clambered straight back out, my shirt wet to the armpits, wishing I hadn't. I turned to give Pete a reassuring wave but he'd gone back inside.

We made our way through the knee-deep water along Mrs Melchiori's front fence. At the corner the stormwater drain was marked by a whirlpool and an intermittent high-pitched sucking sound.

Shoe Street was submerged too; the houses on each side seemed to tilt into the water like sinking ships. The witch's place, which was only one storey, had water halfway up its front door.

Connor splashed on down the middle of the road. Where Shoe Street met the street behind ours, which was Byron's street, we were already waist deep. Down the far end of Byron's street a few single-storey houses had only their roofs above water.

As we neared the Harmisons' place Connor began to speed up. 'Bloody hell!' he said and started wading towards the gutter.

'What is it?' I said.

When he got to the Harmisons' front fence he reached down with one arm and began frantically feeling around.

'What are you doing?'

He said, 'Come and help me.'

I made my way across to him. 'Help you what?'

'I put Mum's necklace here yesterday.'

'What? Why?'

''Cause then if Stevie took it I could call the police and tell them to search his place.'

'Great plan,' I said sarcastically.

'I didn't know it was going to flood, did I?'

'It probably got washed away,' I said.

'Aaron, just come and help me look for it.'

It was too deep for me to reach the ground, so I took a breath, and closed my eyes and duck-dived. I felt along the grass but I didn't find the necklace.

When I came up for breath Connor was looking at me. He was puffing. He said, 'He took it. I bet he took it.'

'What are you gunna do?' I asked.

He started to head for the gate to Stevie Harmison's house.

'Connor, don't,' I said.

'What? I'm getting Mum's necklace back.' He climbed the stairs and rang the doorbell and waited, with his arms folded in front of his chest.

'They're not home, Connor,' I shouted to him.

He knocked, tried the doorknob. Looked through their front window. Rang again. He pulled at the window to see if it would open. It didn't. Then he came back down the stairs.

'What now?'

'I'm going to Damon's. I'll check again on the way back.'

But Damon's house was still a long way—as far as an island from a beach.

I said, 'It's gunna get deeper, you know.' Connor was a bad swimmer—worse than me.

'So?'

'So we might have to swim. What if there's snakes in there or something?' The *something* that had popped into my mind was from the rainfish story. But I couldn't tell Connor that—he'd think I was being an idiot.

'If it gets too deep you've gotta turn back,' said Connor. 'And you have to promise not to get in the way.'

'But Pete said—'

He cut me off with 'I don't care what *he* thinks.' And he started wading down Shoe Street again, and after a moment's hesitation I went too.

We kept to the centre of the road. The going got tougher and the water got colder with every step. Before I knew it I was in up to my belly button. Connor kept on determinedly, not looking back to see how I was going.

When the water was up to my chest I said, 'Connor,' and he stopped with a sigh.

We were more than halfway. Damon's house was looming. Connor didn't take his eyes off it. 'You can go back, but I'm keeping on going,' he said.

I started to swim, breaststroke, keeping my chin well up out of the water. It felt weird to swim down a road I had walked along so many times.

Soon Connor began to swim as well.

After a while he could walk again. Then I could too.

'Wasn't that bad,' I said, but I was panting.

Connor nodded, panting too. 'Easier than I thought it'd be,' he said.

Damon's place had water halfway up its stilts. Wet sheets were draped over the front stair rail and more were piled on the veranda.

Connor called out, 'Anyone home?'

No answer.

A loud splash, and laughter, drifted from the back-yard. As soon as Connor heard it he called, 'I'm comin' round, Damon,' and he began to wade through the chest-deep water along the side of the house.

I followed, and in that way we arrived at Damon's backyard—or rather the place Damon's backyard had once been. Now it was a giant muddy swimming pool. Beyond the back fence, of which only the tips of the star pickets were showing, stretched an inland sea. The swamp was somewhere beneath it.

Connor and I perched ourselves on Damon's back stairs and caught our breath. Damon was swimming breaststroke near the back fence. Stevie Harmison was there too, doing some sort of backstroke.

'Perfect,' Connor whispered when he saw Stevie.

Coldy was there as well. Now I knew why he hadn't come pestering me for ages. What Stevie and Damon were thinking in letting a kid like him hang around them I had no idea—maybe he'd shown them his worm-eating act. Anyway, there he was, swimming behind Stevie like he was his puppy, and looking at me like he didn't recognise me now that he was *so* cool.

Connor called out, 'Damon.'

Damon turned round and looked right at me, but just said, 'Connor. Didn't see you there. What d'ya think of me pool? Mad, ay? It's so deep at the back I can't hardly even *touch*.'

'Aren't you worried about crocodiles?' asked Connor.

Stevie said, 'Oh yeah, *real* worried.' He started splashing and waving his arms about, yelling, 'A croc's got me. Save me, Damon.'

Damon and Coldy laughed.

Connor eased himself into the water and started to swim around.

'I'm going again,' Damon said to the others.

'Where?' asked Connor.

'You'll see.' He swam to the steps and brushed past me as he made his way up to the veranda where he climbed onto the handrail.

'Yodelay hee-hoo!' he yelled. Then he jumped, curled into a bomb and smashed the water causing a tidal wave that kept going past the fence and into the swamp.

'Cool,' said Connor who was dogpaddling in little circles in the deeper bit like he was proving he wasn't afraid of crocodiles. He had to lift his chin to avoid swallowing Damon's wave.

Damon rubbed his eyes and shook his glasses dry.

'Have a go, Connor. We've all done it.'

'Yeah, maybe.'

'You should have been here before. Dad caught a black bream right there off the veranda.'

'Yeah?' said Connor. He'd swum over near Stevie. He said, 'How's it going, Stevie?

Instead of answering Stevie laughed and shook his head.

'Did you happen to see a necklace out the front of your house?' asked Connor.

'A necklace? You wear necklaces, do ya?'

'No. But *you* like necklaces, right? And beads?' said Connor.

Stevie sighed. 'Why'd you invite Frenchie?' he said to Damon.

'Who?'

'This bloke.' He grabbed Connor around the neck. A wrestler's chokehold. He bared his teeth as he did it. I couldn't see Connor's face, just his chin. He was splashing around and trying to keep his head out of the water.

'I didn't,' said Damon. 'He lives down the road.'

Connor was trying to pull Stevie's arm away from his neck.

Damon said, 'Why do you call him Frenchie?'

'He reckons he can speak French.'

Connor managed to say, 'I never said that.'

'Can you speak French?' asked Damon.

'I never...said I could,' Connor spluttered.

'Go on, say something French, Frenchie,' said Stevie, and he pulled on Connor's neck.

Connor's splashing became more frantic. 'Let me go,' he cried out.

Stevie dunked Connor's head underwater. Connor came up coughing and taking big drawing breaths.

I said, 'Let him go.'

'I think he wants one more,' said Stevie, and he dunked him again.

When he came up, Connor was gasping and splashing and fighting, but Stevie was a lot bigger, and he just laughed.

Connor said something, I think it was *Piss off*, or it might have been an attempt at some French, which, of course, he couldn't speak.

I yelled out, 'Let him go.'

'Want a go, Damon?' Stevie said to Damon.

'Nah,' yawned Damon.

'I won't have a go either just yet,' said Coldy with a guffaw, and at that moment I hated him more than any of them.

With his free arm, Stevie pretended to punch
Connor in the head, three big punches, and he yelled
'Bam' with each fake punch: 'Bam! Bam! Bam!' Then
he dunked Connor one more time and as he did he
pushed him away.

'Go put on ya necklace, ya little girl,' he sneered.

Connor surfaced and swam slowly back to the
stairs. His eyes were red and he was coughing. I tried
to help him up but he shrugged me off. Once he was
firmly on the stairs he turned and kicked water at
Stevie but it hardly even reached him.

Damon and Stevie and Coldy all laughed.

'Off ya go, Frenchie,' said Stevie.

'Back to France,' added Damon. They laughed
again.

'I'm gunna see if I can touch out the back,' said
Stevie, and he and Coldy swam towards the back fence.
But Damon didn't—he stayed standing chest-deep in
the dirty water. He'd seen the look I'd given him, and
had stopped laughing.

He said, 'What are *you* looking at?' bristling like we
were two cowboys at high noon, like the way Graham
Boon had just before he threw the punch that had
started the only fight I'd ever been in.

Connor said, 'Ignore him,' and he began to climb

off the stairs, turning his back. And at that instant Damon's bully-boy expression switched off, and he mouthed 'Come back later.'

It happened so quickly and was so unexpected that I couldn't do anything but stare at him.

'Go on, piss off,' he said. Connor was looking again; bully-boy Damon was back.

'Get stuffed,' said Connor, but Damon had begun swimming towards the others, who were duck-diving for the bottom like they'd already forgotten we were there. *Come back later*—he meant when Connor had gone. 'Don't count on it,' I said under my breath. 'You two-faced bastard, you piece of shit.' And then I followed Connor back around to the front of the house.

16

MURKY WATER

CONNOR AND I stood in Damon's front yard contemplating Shoe Street. In the time we'd been at Damon's the water at the T-intersection had risen. It had been still before, but now it seemed to be moving, flowing past Damon's place towards the swamp.

Connor hadn't said anything since we left Damon's.

'Stevie's a dickhead,' I tried, but he didn't reply. His breathing sounded wheezy, which I knew was a sign an asthma attack might be coming on. He was limping for some reason, and his back was bent like an old man, as he made his way slowly into the water.

'You should've punched him,' I said.

'Like to see *you*,' he replied quietly.

The water began to deepen. I brushed against something soft and heavy and a wave of panic pulsed through me—but it was only a plastic bag full of sopping baby clothes. I threw it as far as I could.

'Are you okay to swim?' I asked.

'Are *you*?' he snapped back.

I started to swim, and when the water was up to his chest Connor did too. We were side by side, going slow, the current gently pushing us sideways.

We swam harder. Connor was struggling, breathing hard.

There was something down there. I knew it. It was the *whatever-it-was*. It swam under us and off, quick as a shark, towards the swamp. But just as quickly it was back, hovering below me. I looked down but I couldn't see the bottom, couldn't see anything, couldn't see its shape, just bony hands that snatched at me.

'Holy shit!' I screamed out. 'It's under me!'

'What? Shut up, Aaron. You're freaking out,' said Connor between panting breaths.

'There's something there. It's grabbing me.'

Don't look down into the water, just keep your head up, I was telling myself. The grey sky and the street spun around me. An old man wearing nothing but a pair of droopy white Y-fronts was standing on the porch of one of the houses, his jaw working like a cow chewing cud. He hardly looked capable of walking let alone swimming out to save us.

I felt something touch my ankles, and that was when I completely panicked, when I stopped swimming and my arms just started thrashing at the water like I thought I could fly out of it.

And I was grabbing Connor and he was shouting, 'Shit Aaron, stop it. Get off me.' But I wasn't doing any of it on purpose.

'You're drowning me, dickhead.'

Anyone watching must have thought we were fighting. Connor was shaking me. He said, 'You're okay,' between breaths. 'Calm down. Okay? Calm down.'

My feet were kind of tingling, but I couldn't feel anything swimming under me anymore. *Just stop thinking about it. Stop thinking about anything.* I wanted to slap myself in the face to calm me down, like they do in old movies.

Just keep breathing, I told myself. I took some deep breaths. Felt myself getting calmer.

By that time Connor had let me go and was treading water. 'You good?' he said.

'Yep,' I managed to say. 'I'm fine.'

My arms were getting tired but we were halfway down the street now, and out of the current, and I sensed the road looming underneath us. Connor kept stopping and trying for the bottom with his feet. Then he could stand, though he had to swim a while more before it was shallow enough for him to walk. I kept swimming, then tried for the bottom and found it too, and I was so relieved I thought I'd cry. Soon we were sloshing through the hip-deep water.

At the corner the whirlpool over the stormwater drain had disappeared and there was no sucking sound. Which meant it was blocked. I knew then that the flood was going to get worse.

'Hey, don't come in here all wet,' said Pete as we walked into the lounge room.

Connor chose that moment to have a violent coughing fit. With each cough his whole body shook, spraying water all over the floor, couch and coffee table. And Mum chose that same moment to appear at the front door.

'Okay, Connor, it's all right, just calm down,' she said as she rushed over to him.

Connor tried to stop coughing and then coughed worse, and Mum hugged him, flattening his face against her chest.

'Jesus, tell me you haven't been swimming in the

street. Pete, you didn't let them go swimming out in the street, did you?' Her eyes were piercing angry.

'Well—' Pete started.

'Did you not *know* he has severe asthma? Connor, go and have a shower. Aaron, you go wait for him then have one too. *Now.*'

Connor had his shower while I stood outside the bathroom. Mum started in on Pete again: '*Tell me* you didn't let Connor go swimming in the floodwater. With raw sewage, with *shit* floating in it. And what about crocodiles and snakes? It's *dangerous*, Peter. Or don't you think at all?'

I couldn't hear Pete's reply.

'So you didn't know he's got asthma, is that what you're saying? That I never told you that?'

Nothing from Pete.

'You're an *adult*,' she shouted.

The bedroom door slammed. The bathroom door opened and Connor brushed past me.

After my shower I went to my room and found Connor curled up on the top bunk with his back to me and not saying anything. Mum was in her room with the door closed, and Pete was in the kitchen playing with the generator, which for some reason had cut out twice already. So I went out onto the front veranda.

The stereo on the veranda of the house across the road was still playing but the couch was empty. And the rain had built up again. It greyed out the houses and slapped into Pete's coffee cup on the gatepost which was in danger of being carried away by the rising water. And now our street was flowing as well, past our place towards Mrs Melchiori's on the corner and down Shoe Street. It felt like it had always been like that, a river slow-flowing and grey-brown, with houses along its banks.

Pete's truck was in it. The water was nearly up to the passenger window. There was water in the cabin. Poor old truck.

I was being punished by the universe. Because of the rosary beads, or because of the rainfish, I didn't know which, but I was definitely being punished. That was why everything was going so disastrously. I couldn't really complain, I deserved it. The question was how much more did I deserve, how much worse were things going to get?

Connor looked pale at dinnertime and he hardly ate anything. No one said much, just 'pass this' or 'pass that'. Mum's face was set in a grim disappointed look, like the world was dark and bad and she'd known it all along and was only now remembering. Pete kept tapping at things. He hit his fork on the edge of the table till Mum asked him to stop.

He cleared his throat. 'Sounds like it's gunna keep this up all night again.'

'Connor, maybe you should go to bed,' said Mum, and Connor didn't argue. Pete tried to take the plates but Mum pulled them out of his hands and washed them herself and then went to her room, leaving Pete and me at the table.

'So what did you two get up to today?' Pete asked with a rueful smile.

'Just went to a friend's house.'

'Yeah?'

'His dad caught a fish off the back veranda.'

'Fair dinkum?' said Pete, looking genuinely impressed.

'Sorry we went so far.'

'Nah,' said Pete. 'Don't worry about it. You can't keep kids in cottonwool. Anyway, you better get to bed too, I s'pose.'

'All right. Night, Pete,' I said.

'Night, mate.'

The light was off when I crept into my bedroom. I got into bed carefully to avoid making it squeak, but then I heard Connor roll over and I knew he was awake.

Mum was shouting again. Pete shouted something back.

'Connor?' I said.

'Yeah?'

I heard something smash. 'I can't sleep.'

'Don't worry. They'll stop soon.'

'Did you ever hear Mum and Dad fight like that?'

'They were worse than this. This is nothing. One time Dad chucked his dinner at the window over the sink and broke it. That's how come the glass in that window's different. You were just a baby. And one time he put his fist through the wall. This is nothing.'

'Do you remember much about him?' I asked.

He took a while before answering. 'He used to do chin-ups all the time. He was gunna teach me how to box.' Connor's voice sounded thin through the mattress. 'He knew how to play chess. He used to go fishing too but I never went with him. He used to fish off the beach somewhere. He got a big one one time. Think it was a sand shark. It was huge. He brought it home. Don't think we ate it though. Think we chucked it out.'

'Mum would probably remember about it.'

'Yeah.'

'Hey, Connor?'

'Yeah?'

'I forgot to tell you. I found *The Lord of the Rings* the other day. I've got it here if you want. You can put my reading light on and read it.'

'Thanks,' he said.

I got up and got the book out of the cupboard and gave him the lamp, and he read. And after a while the sound of fighting stopped and I went to sleep and dreamed about spiders and crocodiles, fish that could bring the rain to help them escape, and the bunyip from the rainfish story. In my dream it was a skeleton monster with skeleton hands. And I dreamt of being dragged under the water, and not being able to breathe.

17
THE MONSTER

CONNOR WAS COUGHING in the bunk above me. The noise woke me up, and the fact that each cough made the bunk shake and was followed by a wheezy, strained in-breath. It was still dark. The rain was still pounding on the roof.

'Connor. Connor, are you awake?'

He answered with another wave of coughing. After the coughing his breathing sounded urgent.

I got up and stumbled into the hall to get Mum. She met me halfway, and I held onto her nightie as I followed her back to our room.

She turned on the light, which made me wince.

'It's all right, Connor. It's okay,' she cooed, and she kissed him on the ear before lifting him off the bed like he was a baby. She carried him to the lounge room and lowered him onto the couch. Pete stood in the hall in his boxers watching as Mum disappeared into their bedroom and emerged with a blanket which she draped over Connor. She also had both his puffers; she held them up in turn and helped him suck in the medicine. Then she began talking quietly to Pete. I heard him say, 'We could get a boat,' and her reply, 'There's no time.' Then she called to me, 'Aaron, can you find the torches?'

Pete pulled on a shirt while Mum rang the ambulance. I stood on a chair in the hall to reach the top of the broom cupboard where our torches were kept. Only one of them worked. I put it on the coffee table and then stepped back and watched Connor. He was sweaty. He was breathing fast, making a high-pitched sound with each breath. Mum came back and said to Pete, 'They told me to wait.' She stood with me, watching Connor.

Then she said, 'Aaron, I want you to stay here while me and Peter take Connor up to the hospital. Okay? You can watch TV if you want.'

I said, 'Okay.' Then I burst into tears.

Mum hugged me.

'It's all right, mate,' said Pete. Then he bent down. 'Come on, Connor,' he said and he picked him up.

Mum switched the torch on and I followed them out onto the veranda. The rain was hammering on the roof, driving into the water. There was no moon or streetlights, no houses had their lights on except for ours, but I could see the water was higher than before, much higher. If it kept rising, soon it would be all the way up the stairs and coming in our front door. And it was flowing much faster. I could hear it moving: a rustle, a murmur.

Connor's head was slumped against Pete's chest. His body was shaking. I wanted to say something to him, but then I lost sight of him as Pete turned towards the stairs. They sloshed down the front stairs. The water was above their hips already.

'Go inside, Aaron,' said Mum. 'We'll be right.'

But I stayed watching. Pete was in up to his chest at the front gate. Soon I couldn't see them, only the beam of the torch inching forwards above the swirling, eddying water. Suddenly I couldn't see it either.

'Mum?' I called. 'Pete?'

They couldn't hear me over the rain and the rustle of the torrent hurrying past. It was a mocking sound, and within it I heard a dripping, hushing voice, coming from out there somewhere, soft as a gust of wind, that I recognised well. '*Why don't you come in and save them?'* It was the thing. *'Come in,'* it called. *'They'll put you in the paper. They'll say, "He went into the flood at night and saved his family. So brave. Such a brave little boy."'*

I went inside. I turned the TV on and flicked through the channels: white noise, test patterns, an old cowboys-and-Indians movie, a woman with bright orange hair and an American accent in front of painted meadows and mountains. I turned up the volume to hear her over the rain: 'Now I'm gunna be talking about sin and forgiveness of sin. Verse thirteen. Is anyone among you afflicted? Ill-treated, suffering evil?' She was reading from a big Bible open on a lectern.

'Don't you want to come swimming with me again? We had fun didn't we?' The thing rose from the gutter and began to circle the house, just beneath the surface, its tail making a bow wave in the black water. *'Stevie Harmison would have gone in to save his family. Maybe even Coldy would have.'* The thing was looking in at the light from the lounge-room window, and the light caught on its teeth and on the black dripping-wet skin of its head.

I changed the channel back to the cowboys and Indians. They were all on horses galloping over a flat desert. I couldn't tell who was chasing who.

The thing was on the front stairs now, with its long tail trailing in the current. *'Have you guessed what I am yet? Why I'm here? I've come here for you. Because of what you've done. I am the consequence.'* I tried not to look over at the door. I tried to ignore it. But it kept calling me: *'Aaron. You're the one I want. Come into the water. I want to talk to the great Aaron Aaronson. Man of the Match. The smartest. The bravest.'*

From the corner of my eye I saw long thin fingers at the open doorway. I saw them grip the floor and push further into the room. *'Come into the water. Or perhaps I'll come in there with you.'* A face was emerging from the darkness, with teeth like a deep-sea fish and staring human eyes.

Don't look at it. Ignore it, I tried to tell myself. I dragged my eyes back to the TV just as a gun fired and the chief Indian fell from his horse. And that was when the power went off. The TV was dead. I was sitting rigid on the couch, the darkness swirling all around me.

It's here. It's here with me.

I thought about Mum and Pete, straining, hand in hand, the water up to their necks, the current prising them apart. Connor's lungs closing. Connor rolling helplessly along under the water, Mum calling, diving, calling again. The thing said, '*I see them*,' and it turned and with a powerful flick of its crocodile's tail it launched into the water and dived, and then crawled along the submerged road, making its way towards them.

The lights came back on.

The Indians were charging through a canyon, the cowboys were hiding among the rocks blazing away with their guns. I looked to the door—no monster, of course. But still I couldn't move from the couch. *You arsehole. You coward*, I thought. But what else could I have done? There was nothing.

I tried to empty my mind. I took everything from my mind and scrumpled it up like a piece of paper and threw it in the rubbish bin. Replaced it with nothingness. A dark void.

But thoughts kept inching back from the darkness, from the edges of my mind. *An ice cream on a sunny day. Soccer in the backyard. The lemon tree. Where do spiders go when it rains? They go inside. They hide in corners and under the couch.* No! *Empty your mind. Focus on the movie.* The cowboys were still shooting. There was only one Indian left. I thought, *There's nothing inside me.* The Indian clutched his chest, he fell backwards off his horse. I shut my eyes tight. Then opened them.

The phone rang.

I ran to it. It was Mum.

'We're at the hospital,' she said. 'The doctor's seeing Connor, Pete's on his way back now. I'm just ringing to check you're okay.'

'Is Connor all right?'

'We dunno yet. I'm gunna stay tonight. Pete should be home soon. You should go to bed.'

'Okay,' I said.

'Okay,' she replied.

I went back to the lounge room and watched TV again.

Half an hour went by before I heard footsteps on the stairs. Pete was back. He came and stood in the lounge room, sopping, making a puddle at his feet.

'Everything's gunna be all right, mate,' he said, picking up a towel that had been left on the floor and wiping his face and arms with it. Water soaked the mat and splattered the TV and the couch and the blanket on it. And I was still sitting watching him like he was a ghost, so sure had I been that neither he nor Mum nor Connor would ever come back.

I said, 'The lights went out.'

'Be the generator playing up again,' he said and he switched off the TV. 'Off to bed now, ay?'

And I went to bed, but I could not sleep, in fact I could not even close my eyes.

18

A CONFESSION

AN ORANGE GLOW was seeping through my eyelids. I fought it for a while, keeping my eyes shut tight. But it was no use. I was awake. I looked out the window; the sky was all white cloud. The rain had stopped.

I crept along the hall and saw that the roof wasn't leaking anymore, but that the bucket Mum had put there was full and the puddle around it was soaking Connor's mattress, which was leaning up against the wall.

Pete was smoking in the kitchen. 'Sorry, mate,' he said, stubbing the cigarette in his coffee cup and flapping his hands at the smoke.

'Have you heard how Connor is?' I asked.

'Nah, not yet,' he replied. 'You want some brekky?'

He made eggs on toast which we ate looking out

at the yard. I kept yawning. The water seemed lower. And lifeless, somehow; just water. When I tried to picture the monster, all that came to me was a sense of unease, as if the night before had been shut behind a door down a long corridor up a flight of stairs in some part of my brain I hardly ever visited.

'What are we going to do today?' I asked.

Pete shrugged.

After breakfast he found a handline, threaded a bit of leftover steak onto the hook and cast it off the back stairs, landing the bait under the clothesline. I sat next to him for a while, but he didn't get any bites.

'Get us a beer while you're up, would ya, mate?'

I got him one and then wandered back to my bedroom. *The Lord of the Rings* was on the top bunk. I opened it, skipped the foreword and the prologue, looked briefly at the maps, then started on page one:

'When Mr Bilbo Baggins of Bag End announced that he would shortly be celebrating his eleventy-first birthday with a party of special magnificence…' I held it up by its spine, let the pages fan out. Looked at the last word on the last page, thinking, *I'll tell Connor I've read it and I'll prove it by telling him the last word.* But it was nothing special, and when I closed the book I immediately forgot it.

We had toast for lunch in front of the TV: '...reports of looting, though no arrests. Continued rain is restricting police attempts to locate a boy swept away in floodwater while apparently swimming with friends late last night. Police spokesman Sergeant Paul Landers has sent a warning to parents.'

Mr Landers, in police uniform and police hat, came on. 'I can't stress enough how important it is that people don't let their kids go swimming in floodwaters. It's just common sen—'

'Your mum might be home soon,' said Pete, talking over the TV. He coughed, and then stood up.

Sure enough Mum came home a little while later wearing a borrowed T-shirt and shorts. She had a strained smile on her face, and she looked at only the things she wanted to look at, and Pete wasn't one of them. She knelt down and gave me a bear hug.

'Are you being good for Peter?' she asked and I said that I was.

'I've just come to get some things,' she said, to both of us, not directly to Pete.

'How's Connor?' I asked.

'They think he's got pneumonia, probably from swimming in dirty water. And together with his asthma it's knocked him around a fair bit. You don't feel sick, do you, Aaron?'

I shook my head. 'Can I visit him?'

'Not yet. He's still too sick. I'm going back up soon. I'll probably come back later tonight. Peter might make you some tinned spaghetti on toast for dinner.'

She hugged me again, kissed me on the forehead and then was gone.

'Might go do a bit more fishing,' said Pete, and then he sat again on the top step and cast his line far out into the yard, right out to near the orange trees.

'Can I go have a look round, Pete?' I asked.

He looked up sharply, then laughed. 'You serious?'

'Honestly, I won't be long. And I won't go in past my knees.'

He turned back to his fishing. After a while he said, 'What the hell. Can't keep kids in cottonwool. Actually, know what?' He threw down his line. 'I might as well come with you.'

Sunlight reflected off the glassy water. It had shrunk from the yards opposite, and from the school oval, but it still covered the road.

There was a line of mud round our house that must have been the high-water mark. It was only a few centimetres below the top stair. Pete's mug was gone from the gatepost. A couch had run aground in our driveway. Its cushions were missing and the springs and wooden frame were exposed.

Pete's truck had a mud line near the top of the windscreen. He waded out to it and opened the door. Water dribbled out. He didn't bother trying to start it.

'Will you be able to fix it, Pete?'

'I'll tow it up to Robbo's and have a look at it in a few days. I bloody knew this would happen, you know? So why didn't I move the thing?' He said this last question in a low voice, more to himself than me.

'What if you can't?'

He hesitated. 'Well,' he said, squinting up the road, 'I might go do a spell on the trawlers. Be good to get out on the sea again. It's good for you, I reckon, the sea. Gives you time to think about stuff.'

We followed the dotted white line that was just visible through the ankle-deep water in the centre of the road, heading away from the Shoe Street intersection. All the houses had junk around their front fences like milk cartons and babies' bottles and plastic cups and esky lids. An old lady was pushing a broom across her veranda, making waves that fell with regular splashes into her front yard while her husband sat on the stairs and watched us go by. Above us flew a V of black-headed ibises.

At the intersection a breeze ruffled the surface of the water. Some of the last houses down the street to our left were single storey and had only their mud-coated roofs showing. We started back the way we'd come.

'Tell me a story about the trawlers, Pete.'

'Like what?'

'What's the weirdest thing you ever caught?'

He thought about it. 'Have to be a port and starboard fish, I s'pose. Got it trolling deep one time. It's basically just a little pineapple with fins. They call 'em port and starboard 'cause they reckon they've got one red light and one green one on 'em. Didn't know what the hell it was. Had to look it up.'

We passed home, then turned into Shoe Street, which was still flooded all the way to Damon's house. The witch's house was half underwater. An uprooted tree was resting on her hedge, its branches were bent against her white walls and one had smashed through her front window. 'Poor bastards,' said Pete. 'They spend their lives thinking about their car, house, mortgage, workin' their guts out all the time, and then something like this happens. What's the point?'

I said, 'I'm not gunna be like that.'

Pete shook his head. 'You got plenty of time to worry about that stuff, mate. When you're a bit older.'

I saw a seagull loop down and pluck at the surface of the water, and I thought about the rainfish. Where were they? Swimming down a muddy drain, or on the road, slipping between our ankles, or exploring the backyards along Shoe Street, swimming in and out of front gates. Or out to sea, pitching in unfamiliar currents.

'I might head back,' said Pete.

'Can I visit my friend? He lives down this street?' I pleaded.

Pete sighed. 'Ten minutes, all right? I mean it.'

'No worries, Pete.'

I sloshed through the street behind ours and found Byron on the front stairs of his place reading an *Archie* comic.

'Byron,' I called.

He gave a start and said, 'Aaron. What are you up to?'

'Just looking round.'

He came off the stairs and we sloshed knee deep through his yard.

I said, 'You got flooded pretty bad.'

'Inside's worse. We got mud all through everything.'

'Fair dinkum?'

'Yep. Bedrooms and everything. I was lying in bed and could reach down and put my hand in the water. Everyone's at my cousin's place. Just Gran and me stayed here last night. All our stuff's all wet. TV's buggered. Come on, I'll show you.'

We went up the back stairs. Inside the house smelled like mud and wet cardboard. There were puddles in the hallway. Their lounge-room carpet was caked with mud. The TV was on a chair.

'Full on,' was all I could think to say.

'Yep. I'm going over to my cousin's place this arvo till it's all cleaned up.'

In the kitchen an old lady was crouched on the floor scraping mud from the lino with a bit of cardboard.

'This is my gran,' said Byron, 'This is Aaron. He lives over the back fence.'

She paused where she was and said, 'How'd you go at your place?'

'Our yard got flooded but our house didn't, except for my brother's room. Your place is really bad.'

She said, 'Yep. There's people down the street who got it worse though. Old Mr Ambrum slept on his roof last night. It'll take a while for everything to dry out. When the water goes down we'll have to air things out. Lots of work to do yet.' She went back to scraping the mud.

Byron said, 'Aaron's the one who was asking about the rainfish.'

She stopped and sat up. Her flowery dress was dirty with mud, she had sweat on her forehead. She said, 'I know people call them mudcod. That's all right. My old mum always called them rainfish.'

'Told ya,' said Byron.

I said, 'Why do they call them rainfish?'

She hesitated. 'There's a story, they say. Don't catch them fish 'cause they'll bring rainstorms and floods and bad things. That's why in the old days people didn't ever eat them.'

I said, 'Do you think the flood happened because we caught them?'

Byron said, 'Nah, it's not your fault,' and Gran said, 'Nah, it's the rainy season. Usually not this rainy but it always rains this time of year. Them fish are bad for you to eat, that's all, make you sick. That's what they reckon anyway. That's why there's stories about them. Make you leave them alone. You emptied out your cupboard, Byron?'

He hadn't.

'Well get in and do it. Go on,' his gran said.

She started scraping again, and Byron said he should go and do his room but he came out on the stairs with me.

I said, 'My brother's sick. He's in the hospital.'

'That's no good,' said Byron, and I kind of felt silly because I hadn't meant to say it, it just came out.

'Anyway, see you later,' I said, and walked back. *Probably they're right*, I thought to myself. *Probably the rainfish had nothing to do with anything. Just me over-imagining, as usual.*

When I got home Pete was on the back stairs fishing. He still hadn't got any bites.

He cooked tinned spaghetti on toast for dinner, which we ate in front of the TV. The news was on. It was about the flood and the missing boy. They said his name was Ross Caulderson, which was Coldy's real name, and all at once I saw how it must have been, how they would have been doing some crazy stunt, the sort of adventurous thing people like Damon and Stevie Harmison liked doing—something tinged with danger. Things like jumping off bridges and stealing stuff and other things that scared the hell out of me. Weird to say, but even though Coldy was missing I felt a tiny bit jealous of him.

I said to Pete, 'I know that boy. He lives just down the road.'

'Yeah?' said Pete, 'That's no good.'

I felt bad. I even tried to squeeze out some tears, but none came. Instead I kept thinking, *Thank God it's not*

Mum or Pete or Connor who's missing. Or me.

After the news we watched *Neighbours*. A girl shoplifted some earrings from a clothes shop, walked right out with them, and she let out a sigh of relief just as the security guard slapped a hand onto her shoulder. I jumped; Pete didn't react. The security guard called the police while the shoplifter rang her brother, crying, and told him what had happened. The ads came on.

'You remember when someone broke into the church?' I said to Pete. 'And took the rosary beads?'

Pete nodded, still watching the TV.

'Well that was me and another bloke.'

Neighbours came back on. A policeman showed up. He knew the girl.

Pete sipped his beer. 'Where are they now?'

'The other bloke's got them. He's the one who *actually* took them. I wanted to take them back but he wouldn't let me.'

'Tricky,' said Pete.

Neighbours ended and the theme song started. Pete looked at me and smiled apologetically. 'Leave it with me, mate. Let me think about it. I'll come up with a plan of action for ya.'

'Thanks, Pete.'

I went to bed. After a while I heard Mum come

home. I heard her voice and Pete's voice. They started arguing again. I tried not to listen but it was hard. I pictured them standing by the kitchen table. And if I walked out there, what then? Would they stop? Mum was screaming now. Something in Pete's tone was egging her on, urging her to get louder. Neither of them cared, they were saying exactly what they wanted, getting it all out. I shut my eyes and blocked my ears and made snoring noises, and tried to fool myself that I was already asleep.

19

THE START OF TERM MASS

FATHER LOCKHART SAID, 'Please stand for the Gospel according to Luke,' and the congregation—a whole churchful including us high school kids and the primary school kids and the teachers and some parents—all stood up. I was careful not to be first or last. Father had been scanning our faces since mass had started and so I'd kept my head in my hymn book or down low as if I was suddenly deeply interested in the graffiti scratched on the pew in front of me.

By then the skies had cleared, and the floodwaters had receded leaving scattered puddles, which then wasted to nothing. The council had collected the couch from our driveway along with all the tree branches and assorted junk from the roads, and the traffic had returned. Connor was home from hospital, and together we'd scraped the mud from his room and he'd moved back in. We walked to school together as we had before, except now I was at the high school too.

During the flood recovery the *Fingleton Gazette* was full of warnings about fallen electricity lines, and pet lost-and-founds and timetables for the council rubbish collections and other flood stories. Then normality returned and so did the interest in criminals like 'Local Man', who'd smashed his neighbour's mower with a sledgehammer, and good old reliable 'Local Youth', who'd been throwing rocks at streetlights. The rosary-beads thieves had been pushed aside for the flood reports and now seemed to have been forgotten.

I was only four rows from the front at the Start of Term Mass and right in the middle of the pew, and I was feeling pretty exposed. The church was loud with whispering and scrapes and coughs.

On the first day back at school everyone in my class had a flood story. 'It was up to *here* in my backyard.' 'That's nothing, in my backyard it was up to *here*.' But most of those kids lived on the other side of town and had got hardly any water, and they were jealous of the one or two kids who had really been flooded. Not many of them knew more about the floods than me—apart from Coldy, that is.

A girl in Connor's class had just finished the second reading. To get to the microphone she'd had to step past a blown-up school photo of Coldy—one of those ones where they make you put your fists on your knees and say 'monkeys'—which had been leant against a chair in front of the altar, with his name and *we will remember you* written under it. The church didn't have flowers or banners because of what had happened to Coldy, and there was a special reading, which was just a big speech about how nice he'd been and how hard it was for his friends in this sad hour, and how we should all support them if they looked like they were upset. Lots of kids turned in their seats towards Stevie Harmison, Coldy's self-appointed best friend, who stared straight ahead like if he did anything else he would burst into tears. He'd been with Coldy when he went missing. 'We were all swimming, it was dark, he was behind us, we turned around and he was gone,' was the explanation he gave. But I remembered Damon's story about his gang, the Evil Deads, who used to go out at night, and I wondered what they'd really been doing. People had spent days looking for Coldy, but they'd found no trace of him.

Damon hadn't ended up coming to our school

after all. In fact, his family had moved out. I knew this because Connor had walked past Damon's place and seen that it was all closed up. Later I overheard Stevie Harmison saying that Damon's grandmother in Townsville had taken the family back.

After the special reading there was a minute's silence for Coldy, during which Father Lockhart rested his hand on top of Coldy's picture like he was comforting a real person. Instead of his special mass robe he was wearing his priest's plain white short-sleeved shirt and black pants, and he looked like he hadn't combed his hair: a few strands were sticking up at right angles to his head.

When we sang 'The Lord's My Shepherd', Father was off key and out of time. He seemed more focused on watching us kids as we sang or pretended to sing or hid behind hymn books.

After the hymn it was homily time. Father bumped the microphone as he took it from its stand but held back from speaking a while, making sure we were all looking at him.

'As we begin today let us first think of the Caulderson family in this time of great loss.' He glanced toward the front pew, but Coldy's family wasn't there. I remembered his mum's cream-cheese sandwiches, how she'd even cut the crusts off. The thought brought with it a pang of guilt.

Father was pacing up and down in front of the altar. He said, 'The holidays were a difficult time for many of us. I've been told it was the worst flood in Fingleton for almost thirty years. Some people were forced to spend a few nights camping in the classrooms, a few of you, I see.' He squinted as he looked out over our faces. I dipped my head further into my hymn book.

'I'm not sure whether many of you know,' continued Father after another dramatic pause, 'that somebody broke into the church over the holidays and stole something very dear to me. Something that had been passed down through my family for generations.'

He's going to point his finger at me and say, 'Thief! I'd know that face anywhere. Stand up. Someone hold him!'

'I know it's only *a thing*,' continued Father, 'but I fell into a funk about it. I even considered resigning.'

There was a murmur among the congregation. The ladies in the front row half-turned to show their disapproval.

'I prayed to God for guidance,' he continued. 'I felt I'd hit a brick wall. And then the flood came. And I was so busy doing things for others I forgot my own problems. Now, I see the flood as a message, to me, from God. And the message was: "Father Lockhart, get to work." So I did. And once I'd started working, I couldn't stop. If you look around you may notice some of the pews have been sanded back and revarnished.'

The first two rows of pews *had* been freshly sanded and revarnished, and they were now a paler colour and shinier than the rest.

'And then,' he said, and suddenly he was trembling with emotion, pointing at the roof with his index finger. And even the kids beside me, who'd been whispering and snickering the whole time, even they shut up.

'While I was sanding, with the sweat upon my brow,' he continued. 'God spoke to me. In a voice sweet and clear, He said, "You will find your father's rosary beads. They are close by."'

A shot of electricity ran through me.

Father kept on, his words slow and deliberate. 'And I was at peace. I believed—I believe it still—that they will be found. They will be returned.'

The church was silent.

Then he seemed to relax back into himself, and after a deep breath he smiled apologetically. 'And I learnt something: that it is in our darkest hour, when the floodwaters are at their highest, that we recognise those things for which we should be truly thankful. For our faith. Even for the simple gift of being alive. So let us pray again for the Caulderson family. Please bow your heads.'

After the homily it was time for communion. One row at a time we stood up and filed down the central aisle. Too late I thought of rushing to the toilet, but that would probably have drawn more attention to me anyway. *Best get it over with. Just look down, and keep quiet,* I told myself.

We shuffled along, drawing nearer to Father. *Why was it taking so long?* And then his moon face was looming over me, saying, 'Body of Christ,' and I heard myself reply, 'Amen.' And I took the wafer and put it in my mouth, and before I could stop myself I was meeting his gaze. He smiled his distracted priest smile and then looked over my shoulder to the next kid.

He'd forgotten me. I was in the clear. I was so relieved I floated more than walked back to my seat, bumped into the kid in front and nearly caused a chain-reaction pile-up.

After the final hymn, Father said, 'Go in peace to love and serve the Lord,' and we filed out of the church then broke into a race for the bag racks while the adults had tea and biscuits with Father Lockhart.

I spent an hour playing handball with the kids who were waiting to get picked up. When the last of them left I walked home.

20

GRAN'S SECOND VISIT

GRAN'S MINI WAS in the drive. She was in the kitchen with a tray of triangle sandwiches and biscuits on the table in front of her, as well as a cup of tea, which she must have made herself because Mum was still at work.

'There you are, Aaron,' said Gran. 'I'd been wondering when you'd get home. Have a sandwich. They're leftovers from mass.'

Connor was at the table, with his mouth full of sandwich.

'I was showing Connor my new shoes. I got them in Rockhampton. Aren't they a knockout?'

They were high heels the same green colour as her dress. I nodded.

'And what did you boys think of Father's homily? "You will find your rosary beads." Have you ever heard anything like it? You know how he was thinking about resigning? Don't say anything to anyone, but I heard he got a reply to his resignation letter directly from *the Pope*, urging him to stay. And he did such a professional job on the pews. Jesus was a carpenter, you know. Oh, he's a rock of strength. What did you think about it, Aaron?'

I hadn't been expecting the question, 'Umm, what? The pews?'

'Father's homily.'

'It was good.'

Gran sipped her tea. 'And the part about him finding his rosary beads—what did you think about that part?'

I said, 'It was interesting.'

She nodded but didn't say anything. But she was getting at something. She took a sip of tea. Then she leaned in, eyes sparkling, and said, 'Now boys, I gave your father your letters. He told me he was very impressed and said what lovely letters they were. He told me to tell you that he loves you both very much and that he'll write a letter back soon.' Then she put a biscuit from the tray in front of each of us and watched as we ate them.

It was while I ate the biscuit that it suddenly hit

me why she'd been asking me about Father's homily. She must have been the lady in the church back when me and Damon took the rosary beads. She must have known it was me all along. I stopped mid-chew and stared at her.

She sensed me staring. She said, 'And what did you boys think about the bit in the sermon where Father talked about repentance for your sins? What did you think about that?'

'I don't remember that bit,' said Connor.

'Connor, would you be a dear and get my bag out of the car for me?' Connor gave her a funny look, but he went.

Gran waited till he was gone, and then she said quietly, 'I won't tell on you if you give them to me.'

I was too shocked to say anything.

She waited, watching me coldly.

'I haven't got them,' I finally stammered. 'Another boy's got them.'

'Are you telling me the truth, Aaron? Really?'

'I am, Gran. I swear.'

She nodded then.

I took a deep breath to calm myself. 'You knew all along,' I said. 'You were the lady in the blue cardigan.'

'Blue cardigan? No, I just happened to see the letter

you wrote to your father. You're so much like him, you know.' She shook her head. 'Once, when your dad was a boy, he broke into our neighbour's place and took some trinkets. It was innocent, really. But I made a mistake; I told his father. And then there was hell to pay. And your dad blamed me for that. He never confided in me again. Never forgave me. And I blame myself. So I won't tell on you, you don't have to worry.'

She sighed. 'He still blames me after all these years. So much anger in him. He still won't see me. Sends my letters back unopened.'

'What about our letters? What about the letter he wrote to me at Christmas?'

She shook her head. 'I wrote that. But I'm sure that's what he'd like to say, if he could. He's just all over the place at the moment. You won't tell Connor or your mother, will you? I want you kids to have a good relationship with him, when he gets back on his feet. He's had it tougher than you. People were always picking on him. And *his* father was so strict. Far too strict, at times. He got mixed up with the wrong people. Listen—I won't tell on you to the police or anyone, but you have to do something for me. You have to confess to Father Lockhart. You have to get your soul right with God. Otherwise, well…I'm giving you a chance, though God knows no one gave your dad a chance. But oh, he was the sweetest little boy you ever saw…'

Gran was still smiling to herself thinking about Dad as a kid when Connor came up the back stairs. 'Did I ever tell you boys about the time your dad was one of the wise men in the school concert?'

We listened to Gran's story even though we'd heard it before. Then we stood on the front veranda and waved as she reversed her Mini out of the driveway. She gave a brief smile up at us, then her eyes went back to the rear-view mirror, and she was gone.

'I heard what she said,' said Connor. 'I was on the stairs. So it was you all along. Pretty sly.'

I stared at him.

'It's okay. I'm not gunna tell. But I wouldn't tell Father Lockhart. You never know what he'll do. Don't tell anyone. It can be our secret.' He patted me on the shoulder.

I said, 'Okay,' and I felt a weight lift off me.

'Just don't do it again, okay?'

I nodded emphatically. 'Definitely not.'

21

THE LAST RAINFISH

THE FIRST SATURDAY after we'd gone back to school, Mum got me to mow the yard. I shoved the mower through the thick grass, with sweat getting in my eyes and the engine's thrum drowning out everything. My hands were throbbing from the push bar.

'After that you can clean out that old tub,' said Mum. 'I'm sick of looking at the damn thing.'

I emptied the grass-catcher's last load behind the chook pen. The spider wasn't there—another victim of the flood, probably—and gone with it was the corner's scary vibe. The bathtub was clogged with branches and weeds, and flies buzzed around it. It stank. I cleared out the big branches then felt around for the plug and pulled it out. Not much water drained, so I got a bucket and began to bail.

Something moved in there. At first I thought I'd imagined it, but there it was again. I saw a fin. I moved the bucket around, trying to scoop it up. Suddenly there it was in the bottom of the bucket, brown against the white plastic, its fins undulating. The last remaining rainfish.

I ran upstairs. 'Mum, I got a mudcod. It was still in the bathtub.'

'You're kidding. That's amazing, Aaron.'

'What should I do with it?'

'You could put it in a tank.'

'Can I go and ask Pete what he thinks?'

She leant back against the sink and brushed a hair from her eyes. She smiled and said, 'All right. Sure. But don't be long.'

'Great.'

I got the bike and rode towards town, keeping well off the edge of the road to avoid the bustling Saturday-morning traffic. It didn't take me long to get to Robbo's workshop. And there was Pete, arms striped with grease, talking to a customer.

Pete had moved out of our place a week after the flood and he was sharing a flat with one of his fishing buddies. He'd sold his truck to a sugarcane farmer who'd put it in his back shed and was fixing it on weekends. The day after Pete left, Bernie came round on his motorbike with beer from his bottle shop, put his feet up on a kitchen chair and started gossiping like nothing had changed.

When Pete saw me he smiled and wiped his hands on his overalls.

'Good to see ya, mate. How ya been? How's Connor and your mum going?'

I told him they were well and he nodded and frowned like we were two men talking business.

Then I said, 'Hey, Pete, guess what? I cleaned the bathtub out and there was a mudcod still in there.'

'Yeah? Who'd a thought it, ay?'

'What should I do with it?'

He squinted at the open workshop door. 'Mate, you should probably take him back to where we got 'im.'

'Okay. Yep. Good idea.'

'Listen mate, I've got a fair bit of work on this morning so I better get back to it, but it was good seeing ya, ay? Thanks for dropping in. And say hello to your mum and Connor for me.'

'No problem. See you, Pete.'

'Take care, mate.'

But as I rode home I began to see how impractical it would be to take the fish back to the rainforest pond where we'd caught him; after all we still didn't have a car. Better to take him to the swamp behind Damon's place and release him there, I thought. So when I got home I balanced the bucket on my handlebars and set off.

I turned into Shoe Street. It was back to its usual self, though you could still see the high-water mud line halfway up the doors of the houses of people who hadn't bothered cleaning it off. The street behind ours was back to normal as well. I'd walked past Byron's place a few times, and I'd thrown some baby oranges at the back fence, but he hadn't reappeared. I asked Mum if she knew anything about the family over the back fence, but she just shrugged.

Coldy's front door was closed. It had an air about it like it never wanted to open again, or maybe it looked the same as usual and the *air* thing was just in my head.

Likewise the witch's place was closed: it didn't look scary at all anymore. When I asked Mum about her, she said that she was Mrs Contarino and that she used to run an Italian restaurant in town and that she was ninety-two and she had been inside the house through the whole flood. She'd managed to get up on her kitchen table and had sat there while her kitchen filled up with water and all her things floated off, and she hadn't eaten for days, and eventually someone had thought to check on her and she'd been taken to hospital while Connor was there, dehydrated and nearly dead, but they'd got her better and now she was in an old-people's home.

The Harmisons' house was completely mud free. A brand new dirt bike was parked under it.

As I rode slowly, carefully along on that cloudless, perfect day I thought about Father Lockhart's homily, how he'd thought the flood had been a message to him—kind of like *he'd* caused it. I still had the feeling that maybe we'd caused the flood when we caught the rainfish. Or maybe Damon and I really had made the universe or something angry when we'd taken the rosary beads. Everything had gone wrong since then. I wondered how many other people felt like they'd caused the flood. Most likely the flood was no one's fault; most likely it was just what happened.

Damon's house was deserted. They hadn't cleaned it at all; there was a mud coating ten centimetres thick under the house and muddy boxes lying about the yard. A dirty sheet was hanging off their front veranda rail.

I left the bike next to the road and trudged through the vacant lot with the bucket. The ground there was still soft.

As I arrived at the clearning I heard the rustle and scurry of small things departing. The creek water was higher and cleaner than it had been. I poured Aaron Aaronson in—I liked to think that it was Aaron Aaronson that had stayed in the bathtub while all the others had swum away. He darted straight for the reeds and was gone.

I straightened up and looked around. There was a prayer card in the mud, bent and soggy. I picked it up. The guardian angel's face still had that weird look, only now, wet and slightly warped, she looked like she was creeping up behind the children, like she was about to push them off the cliff. And there in the reeds, only a metre from me, was the bottle of wine. I fished it out of the mud and wiped it off. It was unopened. The drainpipe, our hiding place, had a dangling tongue of green slime at its mouth, and over the tongue fell a timid trickle of water.

Something caught the light far inside the darkness in the drain.

I reached my arm in. All the way to my shoulder and stretched a little further. I felt something. I pulled:

out came a piece of fishing line with a rusting hook on the end. It glinted in the sun as it turned from side to side. Lucky I'd grabbed the line and not the hook: I might have cut myself and got tetanus.

I peered into the drain again because I had a feeling there was something else up there. Maybe I could reach it if I crawled in a bit. I'd probably fit. There was no point being chicken about it.

'*I wouldn't do that*,' said a voice.

'What? Why not?' I said.

'*Because you don't know what might be in there, that's why. Whatever it is you might not like it.*'

'What's in there?'

The black panther right behind me didn't answer, but the way it was breathing, really fast, and the way the hair on the back of its neck was standing up was starting to concern me.

I thought about it for a bit more, but in the end I took a step backwards and I scrambled up the dirt bank and then walked and didn't run back through the tall grass and through the vacant block.

I got on my bike and rode home and then I went over to Oliver West's house and we played with his remote-control cars all afternoon. Then Oliver came over my house and Mum made spaghetti for dinner, and me and Oliver and Connor and Mum watched TV till late, and Oliver slept over in the top bunk.

I stayed away from the swamp after that day, and from rainfish. And from then on, maybe coincidentally, the panther stayed away from me.

ACKNOWLEDGMENTS

Thanks and love to my family and especially to Megumi and Naomi for supporting and being patient with me throughout the ages that it took me to write *Rainfish*. Thanks to Duncan and Mum and Linda for reading early versions of the manuscript, and thanks to everyone at Text Publishing and especially to Jane Pearson for all her sensible suggestions.